W

FOUNDATION
OF
THE LAW

FOUNDATION
OF
THE LAW

•

Johnny D. Boggs

AVALON BOOKS
NEW YORK

PRINTED IN THE UNITED STATES OF AMERICA
ON ACID-FREE PAPER
BY HADDON CRAFTSMEN, BLOOMSBURG, PENNSYLVANIA

For Butch, Carol and Kent—
and the Summer of '78

So the carpenter encouraged the goldsmith, and he that smootheth with the hammer him that smote the anvil, saying, It is ready for the soldering: and he fastened it with nails, that it should not be moved.

—Isaiah 41:7

As the whirlwind passeth, so is the wicked no more: but the righteous is an everlasting foundation.

—Proverbs 10:25

Chapter One

He opened the new deck of playing cards, glancing at the two one-cent proprietary tax stamps before tossing the wrapper aside, and began shuffling. Frank Ivy hated new cards, disliked the way the ivory finish felt in his hands, how the deck didn't want to bend, and he always feared the cards might explode in his hands and send fifty-two pastecards scattering like leaves, resulting in an outburst of laughter aimed in his direction. It didn't happen, though, and Ivy's hands swept over the top card and tossed it across the table, face-down. Then another. The rhythm felt good, and he silently counted until he and his four opponents each had five cards, the backs reminding Frank of wallpaper.

Not until the other four men picked up their cards

did Ivy place the deck in front of him and look at his own hand. He made no expression, although inside he groaned. Ten of diamonds, queen of diamonds, five of spades, four of diamonds, four of clubs. A pair of fours. Plain old draw poker, high hand. No straights. No flushes. No limit.

The major to his left opened with ten dollars, a substantial amount that caused the whiskey drummer in the bell crown hat to curse, shoot down his glass of rye, and call. The merchant tossed in ten dollars in greenbacks, then added ten more, resulting in another stifled curse from the drummer, who turned in his chair and begged one of the onlookers to bring him another drink. The mule skinner, sitting next to Ivy, folded.

Which is what Ivy should have done. Instead, he called. It was only money, he thought, although he hoped the major wouldn't raise. No luck. The Yankee officer upped the bet another ten, and the drummer, still waiting for his fortitude, pushed in his last chips. After first glancing at his cards, next across the table at the cavalryman, the merchant peeled off another piece of paper money, deciding not to raise. The betting came to Frank once more. Pair of fours, Frank thought, but he had won with worse hands. He matched the bet, placed his cards on the table and reached for the deck.

"How many?" he asked the soldier.

"Three," came the answer, and the major tossed his discards onto the deadwood.

Frank eyed the drummer. "Three," he said hollowly. Frank skinned off three more cards.

"Three," said the merchant.

Pairs all around, Ivy thought. He thought about

keeping the ten and the queen but opted to keep the two fours. The three men left in the game were only betting pairs, and he might match up his fours. He didn't. He looked at his new three cards: ace of clubs, ace of hearts and a beautiful blue ace of spades, with an eagle and thirteen stars printed above it and the name of the card manufacturer, L. I. Cohen, below. Frank Ivy had gone from a pitiful pair to a winning hand. No reason. No skill. Just luck. That's why it was called gambling.

"Ten dollars," the major bet. He hadn't improved his hand.

The drummer folded in disgust and left the table, not saying "good night," "thanks for the game" or "that's all for me," just taking his bell crown hat and empty pockets through the batwing doors and into the cool New Mexico night.

"I'll see your ten," the merchant said, "and raise you fifty."

That brought a whisper from the crowd. Ivy considered the gawkers for a second. He had played in some high-stakes games before, but this wasn't one of them, and he had attracted a few crowds at various gaming establishments, but he couldn't figure out why those six or seven men had picked this table to watch. Boredom, maybe. There didn't seem to be a whole lot to do around Cimarron this evening.

"Sixty to me," Ivy said, glad that someone had improved his hand. He pushed in a handful of chips. "Let's make it an even hundred."

The major smiled, adding his cards to the deadwood. "Not for me, boys," he said. "I'll let you two fight it out."

"Forty dollars to me, then," the merchant said. "I'm

feeling lucky tonight. Here's your forty, and one hundred more."

A bystander whistled, and Ivy began to think the crowd hadn't chosen so poorly after all. He began to doubt himself just a little. Could the merchant have matched his pair twice? Four of a kind? What were the odds? He had lost like that before a time or two, but . . . He grinned.

"That's why they call it gambling," he said, and added a mix of gold coin and paper money into the pot. "I call." That cleaned him out. If the merchant won this hand, Frank would have a cold ride out of town and jerky for supper.

The merchant took in his cards one final time before laying them on the table. "Three kings," he said, "with two queen kickers."

Someone applauded the merchant's hand and delivery. But Frank would upstage him. No jerky tonight, he thought. Beefsteak and brandy and some cobbler for dessert, followed by a bath, shave and a feather bed. "Pair of fours," he said, revealing his hand, "and three ace kickers."

"By jingo!" a cowhand said. "Two full houses!" Another loud whistle punctuated the comment.

As Ivy reached for his winnings, the merchant leaned back in his chair and said dryly, "You skin those cards real slick, my friend."

Frank left the money and cards on the table. His chair squeaked as he leaned away.

"What do you mean by that?" he asked. His eyes hardened. The merchant folded his arms, his right hand disappearing inside his broadcloth coat. Ivy lowered his arm, fingers gripping the butt of the revolver resting on his lap, a precaution he had picked up in

Texas. The crowd began to find less interest in the table and backed to the bar, and the mule skinner joined them, while the major tried to play peacemaker.

"Lee," he told the merchant. "There's no need in this. It's been a friendly game."

"It was friendly," Lee said. "Until this gent decided to deal from the bottom."

The night had quickly turned into one of those evenings every professional gambler dreads. A bad loser spoiling a winning streak. A gambler could cut his losses and leave his money, but then he had best find another profession. Or he could defend himself, and perhaps die in the process. It was another type of gambling, and Frank Ivy never liked those kinds of odds.

"Mister," he said evenly, "I don't cheat." He had almost said, "That's a lie," but stopped himself. He had seen men killed for saying less.

"I say you are," the merchant went on. "I say you're pretty sharp with that new deck."

"You asked for the deck, Lee." The major had stated this, and the merchant's eyes glared at the officer. Still trying to keep the peace, the Yankee went on: "Come on, Lee, forget it. I'll buy you a drink. Let's go."

With a lethal smile, the man named Lee said, "I'll buy our drinks, O'Brien . . . with my money."

His left hand slowly crept toward the chips, coin and paper money, but his right hand remained behind the coat's lapel, and Ivy's and Lee's eyes locked on each other.

"Don't," Ivy said.

The left hand froze about six inches over the table. No one breathed. Major O'Brien decided the time had come to retreat, and he disappeared out of Ivy's vision.

So this is how the night would be remembered. Ivy would kill the merchant, or he'd get killed. One man would be planted in Cimarron's Boot Hill and be talked about as the gent whose luck ran out at Murray's Place until somebody else got killed, and then both tonight's winner and loser, the living and the dead, would be forgotten.

Ivy heard the footsteps. The men who had retired toward the bar, out of the line of gunfire, parted, and a tall figure in fringed buckskin britches and unbuttoned jacket, black hat and gray bib-front shirt made a beeline to the poker table. The man leaned forward, placing two big hands flat on the felt cloth, and said in a thick Texas drawl: "You two boys interrupted my poker game, and it ain't every evenin' that I get a hand like I had. But instead of bettin' up their sorry hands, them boys skedaddled like the Yanks done at Chancellorsville."

"Mister," Lee said, never taking his eyes off Ivy, "this isn't your affair."

"It's my affair when I'm holdin' four jacks." He looked at the cards still on the table. "Thunder, boys, I'da beaten both of you, too."

Lee's face began to flush. "I advise you to stay out of this. This man cheated, and I aim to take what is rightfully mine." The merchant's left hand dropped onto the table, but the man in buckskins moved like a snake. One second his right hand had been flush against the table, and an instant later it crushed Lee's hand.

With a yell, Lee jerked a Sharps four-barrel pepperbox from his coat, but Frank Ivy had his revolver up, hammer cocked, the barrel resting on the edge of the table, aimed at the merchant's face. "Let it drop," Ivy said.

The merchant hesitated only for a second. The hideaway gun fell beneath the table and made a solid thunk on the sod floor. Ivy lifted the barrel up, tugged slightly on the trigger and gently lowered the hammer before standing and shoving the .44 into his holster.

Lee sat like a puppet, unmoving, hard eyes still fixed on Frank, until the newcomer lifted the merchant's limp left arm and said, "The problem here is that we got a cheater accusin' an honest gambler of cheatin'." Lee's eyes darted, and the man in buckskins fingered three cards from the merchant's coat sleeve.

A murmur rose up from the crowd, and the Texan shoved Lee's left arm away as if it were suddenly burning hot. He had surprising strength, and the move caught Lee off-guard, sending him sprawling on the floor. Laughter was cut short when the merchant dived for the pepperbox pistol he had dropped, but the man in buckskins moved quickly, like a cougar. His boot shot up, caught Lee in the middle of his face—a short scream drowning out the sickening crunch—and sent him rolling across the dirt until he slammed against the kegs of whiskey stacked on the far wall. The merchant tried to lift himself, blood pouring from his busted nose, and collapsed, shuddered and lay still.

Turning toward the crowd, the Texan shouted gleefully, "Boys, I don't know what y'all do to cheaters in these parts, but down in Texas, we'd tar and feather the rapscallions and run'm out of town on a rail!"

The consensus sounded almost unanimous. Someone cut loose with a Rebel yell, and the men, once so bored they stood around watching a dull poker game, charged across the room, lifted the unconscious merchant and carried him into the darkened streets. Major O'Brien, still the peacekeeper, ran behind them yelling, "Stop. Don't do it. This isn't right." But Frank doubted if he would have much success.

Ivy gathered his winnings, stuffing coin and cash inside his coat pockets and raking the chips into his weathered slouch hat. Spotting Lee's little Sharps, he picked up the gun and tossed it into a nearby brass spittoon. Murray's Place was almost deserted. A couple of old-timers, who had probably seen enough tar-and-featherings to get excited by any more, sat at a corner table, concentrating on a game of dominoes, and the tall bartender with a bushy black mustache and no left ear, poured the buckskin-clad gambler another drink. Outside, the crowd's cheers and the major's pleas for mercy began to fade.

Hat in hand, Ivy crossed the floor and dumped the yellow, red and blue wooden chips on the plank that served as a bar. "I'd like a whiskey," Frank said, "and to cash these in."

With a slight nod, the barman topped off a relatively clean shot glass in front of Ivy and walked to the other end of the long plank to fetch his cash box. Ivy pulled on his hat and took his whiskey. The other gambler, glass in hand, turned to face him.

Ivy raised his drink in salute. "Hello, Sam," he said.

"Frank," the Texan said, lifting his own glass. "It's been a spell."

Chapter Two

"**D**id you know he was cheatin'?" Sam Raintree asked after slopping up juice from his steak with the last bit of biscuit. He tossed the soggy piece of flour into his mouth and washed it down with bitter coffee, waiting for Ivy's reply.

"No," Frank answered honestly.

The Texan nodded. "Figured as much. Not much of a cheater, though. Most folks would hide aces. This one hid kings."

"He asked for a new deck," Ivy said. "And I was dealing."

Arching his eyebrows, Raintree considered this for a minute. "Maybe he was better than I thought. Ask for a new deck to make it look like he thinks you're cheatin', in case you both show up with a bunch of

10

kings. Or maybe he had the new deck planted—that's more likely—and had taken those kings out of the deck and resealed it. That's pretty smart."

"But he still got caught."

A Mexican waitress came by with two bowls of peach cobbler and a coffee pot. She refilled both men's mugs before leaving. Raintree had polished off his dessert before Ivy had taken two bites. He fingered a toothpick from his hatband and began picking his teeth, waiting patiently for Ivy to finish.

"What's it been?" Frank asked after swallowing the last spoonful of cobbler. "A year?"

Raintree reached for his coffee mug with a shrug. "I don't recollect. What year is it?"

Frank laughed. "1869. Let's see, the last time was March of '68, San Antonio. Pretty much the same deal as tonight. Only . . ."

With a grin, Sam Raintree finished the sentence. "Only there was a bunch of sore carpetbaggers callin' me a cheater and threatenin' to dress me with tar and feathers. And it was you who stepped in, sayin' they had ruined your poker game. One difference, though."

"What's that?"

"I was cheatin'."

Ivy almost spilled coffee. He stared in disbelief, wondering if Raintree was funning him. "You?"

The Texan shrugged. "Bunch of carpetbaggers. Figured they deserved to be cheated. They sure was cheatin' honest folks down home."

They had first met at Appomattox Court House in Virginia. First Lieutenant Franklin Aloysius Ivy, late of the Sixth Virginia Cavalry, and Samuel Dale Raintree, a captain from the bloodied First Texas Infantry, two former Confederate soldiers waiting for their parole papers and passing the time playing poker with a bunch of bluecoats from Michigan.

"This is how we should have fought the War to begin with," Raintree said as he raked in the pot after winning his third consecutive hand.

A Yankee second lieutenant, his cheeks still blackened and scarred from an ugly pistol wound, shook his head and smiled. "I don't think so, Captain."

Raintree looked up, puzzled. "Why not?"

The officer pointed a bony finger and the pile of money in front of Sam, then at Ivy's winnings. "The Union would be asking you Rebs for terms if that had been the case," he said.

Frank and Sam, the only two Confederates in the game, joined the Michiganders in laughter.

Their next meeting came a year later in Fort Smith, Arkansas, again at the same poker table. Frank sat down with fourteen hundred dollars in his money belt, fresh off a winning streak in Memphis, Tennessee. He left with ninety-seven, the worst thrashing he had ever been handed. Sam Raintree, who must have pocketed close to five thousand that night, bought Ivy supper at a cafe overlooking the Arkansas River and gave him this advice: "Frank, there's times to attack and there's times to withdraw, just like they taught us in the War. You was overmatched tonight. You shoulda pulled out early. Cards just weren't comin' your way. It happens."

Ivy took that with him. He learned to pick and choose his games. If the cards weren't coming or if he didn't like the way others played, he'd excuse himself and find another table, or call it a night. He learned to play a mostly conservative game. He might not win a lot of money, but he'd never lose that much—well, most of the time. He had taken some hard hits with good hands, but a gambler couldn't do much about that. He also learned to read his opponents. Drunks played wildly. Cowboys played as if they knew they were going to lose. He developed an eye for cheaters, although he had missed the merchant Lee's moves.

Other habits he picked up in places like Baxter Springs . . . St.   Jo . . . New   Orleans . . . Tucson . . . Denver . . . He didn't like the odds at roulette, never cared much for keno, and lacked the knack for faro, so he stuck to poker. He never overstayed his welcome in any town, even when his winning streak showed no sign of ending and fools filled the gaming halls acting as though they hoped someone would take their money.

In Franklin, Texas, two cowhands got into an argument with each other at Ivy's table. Both men stood and jerked their revolvers, and when the smoke had drifted away, the two cowboys lay writhing on the floor, staining the planks with their blood before dying. After that, Frank began placing his Dance .44 on his lap whenever he sat down for a night of cards.

That safeguard saved his life in Fort Hays, Kansas, in the spring of '67 when a Yank soldier took exception to losing with a a high two pair to three deuces. It had been much the same as at Murray's Place, only that time the soldier didn't stop and Frank pulled the trigger.

He had killed Yankees before, at close range, too, at Brandy Station, Yellow Tavern, Sayler's Creek and other blood-stained fields in Virginia, but this had been different. This hadn't been a war, but a sporting game, a pastime for some, a profession for himself.

Frank often wondered how he had become a gambler.

A native of Virginia's Shenandoah Valley, he had been born in New Market in 1838, the fourth of five children reared by Alexander and Patricia Anne Ivy. Patricia Anne was known as a devout Presbyterian who doted on her three girls and made the best corn pone and ham in the Massanutton Mountains. Alexander Ivy was a carpenter and traveled up and down the Valley Turnpike with a wagonload of tools, building churches, barns and houses as well as chicken coops, cabinets and coffins. His mother often said Frank could drive a nail before he could walk. That wasn't the gospel, but by the time Frank was six years old, he was traveling with his father and older brother, Wilbur, doing menial jobs at first before finding himself on the rafters or digging foundations with Alexander and Wilbur, sweating in the broiling Virginia summers and freezing in the frigid Shenandoah winters.

Oh, Patricia Anne Ivy made sure Frank got an education. She filled the bookcases Alexander had made with Dickens and Balzac, Bronte and Cooper, even *Narrative of the Life of Frederick Douglas, an American Slave* and *Uncle Tom's Cabin*, two works that would have caused a scandal if anyone in New Market learned that a good Presbyterian woman was encouraging her children to read such muck. And she required Frank, Wilbur, Lois, Victoria and Phyllis read a passage from the Bible each night before bedtime.

Alexander Ivy could see the coming war, so instead of going to work for his father as Wilbur had done,

Frank found himself being shipped off to Virginia Military Institute in Lexington. He fared well in his studies, except natural philosophy, and during his final year at the Academy he stood with the other cadets commanded by Professor Thomas J. Jackson and watched the crazed abolitionist John Brown hanged in Charlestown for treason.

When war finally came, Frank was commissioned a second lieutenant in the Sixth Cavalry. Patricia Anne Ivy would never allow playing cards in her house— "the devil's tools," she called them—but his mother remained back in New Market, and Frank's fellow officers taught him the gentlemanly game of chance called poker. Frank learned quickly. Maybe too quickly. He displayed a coolness in battle as well as in the officers' tents for all-night poker games, and usually left with Confederate script and promissory notes from lieutenants, captains, majors, colonels, even two chaplains and one major general. Maybe that was why he only rose in rank to first lieutenant during four years of fighting.

By 1865, Virginia lay in smoldering ruins. Frank could have earned steady work doing carpentry, but he had no taste for it now. His father had left New Market to join that stodgy old professor of Frank's at VMI, who was anything but tiresome on the battlefields and earned the nickname of "Stonewall." Private Alexander Jordan Ivy marched with Jackson's Foot Cavalry until he was killed at Groveton. Wilbur Leo Ivy fell a year later following General Lewis A. Armistead against the Federal center in Gettysburg, Pennsylvania.

His sisters had married—Victoria practically disowned when she wed a captain from Maine and moved to Brewer—and left New Market. Phyllis, a widow after Sharpsburg, was raising a family and being courted by a lawyer in Richmond, and Lois had three children and a hard-working farmer in Staunton. His mother, dead of a broken heart they said, now rested in the cemetery behind the Presbyterian church in New Market, and a Yankee carpetbagger soon occupied the house that Alexander Ivy had built in 1830.

Frank's only ties to Virginia now were his father's silver pocket watch and the fading gray hat he had worn during countless action with Generals Jeb Stuart and Wade Hampton, Colonel Reuben Boston and many other names and faces now forgotten. He was itinerant. His outfit seemed proof of that. His horse, a fourteen-and-a-half-hand palomino mare, came from Savannah, Tennessee. The .44-caliber Dance revolver he had picked up in Texas. He had spent fifteen dollars on his boots, black with red tops inlaid with crescent moons, at cobbler T. C. McInerney's shop in Abilene, Kansas. The spurs had been won off a cowboy down in La Mesilla—when Frank had been bluffing with a jack high. He won the Henry rifle in Sedalia, Missouri, which reminded him that his two previous long guns, a .50-caliber Spencer carbine and an old Enfield musket, had been the casualties of losing streaks, parting his hands in Helena, Arkansas, and Jefferson, Texas, respectively. His saddle came from Denver, gunbelt from San Antonio, and clothes and other traps from various mercantiles and sutlers across the West.

And he was practically friendless. Gamblers seldom made friends. Sam Raintree was an exception. The Texan and Virginian had run across each other a few other times since Fort Smith. They had both lost money on a horse race in Louisville, Kentucky, in the summer of '67 and had sat at different poker tables in Abilene, Kansas, that fall. Two months before their meeting at San Antonio's Menger Hotel, Ivy had taken Raintree for some five hundred dollars in an all-night game in Dallas in January of '68, then watched the Texan, well in his cups, take a vicious pounding by some professional pugilist because of a hundred-dollar wager that no one could remain standing against Man-Killer Roland Beale for two rounds. Raintree's face looked like a slab of steak, but he won that bet.

That was the difference between Sam and Frank. Raintree would lay down money on anything: horse race, shooting match, cards, keno, roulette, boxing, saloon brawl, cockfight, tobacco spitting, or the weather. He'd even bet on how late the train or stagecoach would be running. Ivy usually stuck to poker.

The waitress came by and asked if either man wanted more coffee. Both declined. Raintree slid his toothpick into his hatband and yawned.

"Stickin' 'round here?" he asked.

Ivy shook his head. "That fellow you had tarred and feathered might be a tad angry. Thought I'd try my luck elsewhere. You?"

"Elsewhere sounds good to me. You mind company?"

This surprised Frank. They had known each other for more than four years, but had never ridden together. Even after Appomattox, though both had quickly become friends, they rode out alone, both to discover they no longer had homes. Frank smiled. He would like to share a campfire with a friend for once.

"You have any particular place in mind?" Ivy asked.

"How 'bout E-Town?"

Chapter Three

. . . Blessed are the pure in heart: for they shall see
God.
Blessed are the peacemakers: for they shall be
called the children of God.
Blessed are they which are persecuted for right-
eousness' sake: for theirs is the
kingdom of heaven.
Blessed are ye, when men shall revile you, and
shall persecute you, and shall say all manner of evil
against you falsely, for my sake.
Rejoice, and be exceedingly glad: for great is
your reward in heaven: for so persecuted they the
prophets which were before you.

Ian McKown closed the thick Bible. He glanced at Baldy Mountain to his left, at Scully Mountain to his right and finally looked over the coffin and down the hill at the Sodom springing up before his eyes, an army of canvas tents, dugouts and rough-hewn log cabins. The harsh wind carried up the hill the noise of the bustling community: whines of a sawmill, dull whacks of axes against pine, braying mules, jingling traces, curses, popping whips, a jumbling of loud shouts and conversations, out-of-tune pianos, perhaps a banjo or two, and the falsetto of voices from the dance halls and cribs. Someone had told him that six thousand people had descended upon the Moreno Valley into this mining camp. Camp? Wasn't this the county seat? Yet he wouldn't call what lay before him a town either, nor a city. There might be a few well-built structures, but most buildings lacked a permanence, and the bulk of those six thousand people below him would pack up their tents or abandon their hastily built homes and flee these mountains with the first hard snow.

"Papa?"

He turned, saw his daughter near him, green eyes filled with tears, and behind Alice stood his sons: James, the hothead, and Conall, the strong one, heads still bowed, hats in strong hands. McKown's eyes fell on the casket in front of him. He had built the coffin himself out of pine planks, screwed the hinges on the lid and carved on the top:

WILLIAM WALLACE McKOWN
BORN IN CAMDEN, SOUTH CAROLINA
MARCH 12, 1848
MURDERED IN ELIZABETHTOWN, NEW MEXICO TY.
MAY 30, 1869

Those words would also be put on a headstone ordered from Independence, Missouri, but until that monument arrived, a small wooden cross would mark the final resting place of his youngest son. A father should not have to bury a son, he thought. At least Mary had not lived to see this. It would have broken her heart. McKown passed the Bible to Alice and pulled a piece of folded parchment paper from his frayed black coat. He had spent all night copying a blueprint. Slowly he walked around the hole his sons had spent hours digging yesterday until his calloused hands rested on the pine box, holding the paper down over the hand-carved words. He swallowed, and the hinges squeaked as the lid opened.

"Please," he heard Alice gasp.

Even his sons looked up now.

"This will be for you, William." McKown's lips trembled as he spoke. "This will be your memorial, son. This I promise you." He placed the paper on top of his dead son's folded arms, trying to avoid looking at William's face and neck, and gently lowered the lid. With a nod toward Conall and James, he stepped away and took Alice's small right hand in his own and squeezed it.

"It'll be all right, Papa," she told him.

Conall and James pulled their hats on and picked up the ends of the ropes underneath the coffin. McKown walked his daughter to the other side of William's coffin, where they took hold of the other ends of the lariats. Slowly, they began lowering William into his grave, father and brothers paying close attention to Alice for she lacked their strength. She never complained, never wavered, and with firmly set jaw and determined eyes, concentrated on not dropping the rope or letting the coffin fall too fast.

Back in Camden, perhaps a hundred people would have shown up to pay their final respects for William Wallace McKown. The Presbyterian church wouldn't hold everyone, and afterward the McKown house would be full of friends and neighbors, bringing fried chicken and mashed potatoes, biscuits, pies and cakes, maybe even some sippin' liquor, and they'd share stories about Will, brag about what a fine boy he was, what a good man he would have become and wonder, but never question, the wisdom of God's ways.

Camden, though, lay perhaps two thousand miles east. In Elizabethtown, no one came to see William laid to rest, no stories would be told at the McKown site tonight, and supper would be coffee and warmed-over stew.

When William's coffin hit bottom, Alice and McKown let go of the ropes and stepped back as Conall and James pulled up the sturdy hemp. "You did well," McKown told his daughter, patting her back gently and walking to the mound of dirt on the side of William's grave. He scooped in a spade full and tossed it onto the pine box.

"We'll help you, Father," Conall said and reached for another shovel.

"No," he said tightly. "I'll do it alone. Take your sister back to camp."

Conall knew better than to question his father. Ropes in hands, McKown's two sons guided Alice around the other fresh graves quickly filling the cemetery to the buckboard parked near a small pine. James lay in the back, while Alice sat beside her older brother as he released the brake and popped the reins. The wagon rounded a curve and dipped out of sight.

Ian McKown shoved the spade into the dirt mechanically and dumped another load, slowly covering William for the rest of eternity.

"What was Papa talking about?" Alice said as she began striking a small piece of steel with a chipping claw against flint. Sparks began to shower a thumb-sized piece of charred cloth. When the cloth began glowing and smoking, she grabbed a handful of tinder.

"I don't know," Conall answered. "He was up all night working on something."

"Blueprint," James said.

Alice placed the tinder around the burning cloth and began blowing, fueling and fanning the smoke until the tinder erupted in flames. She added a few small pieces of wood before turning to her brothers.

"Blueprint of what?" she asked.

"I don't know," Conall answered again. "But I imagine Father will tell us when he's a mind to."

She dropped flint and striker into a leather pouch and pulled the drawstring. Alice still found it hard to accept that Will was dead. One afternoon he had been working a sluice box, and that evening he ran from camp to spend his allowance. Joel Lobenstein, who ran the E-Town Mercantile, showed up that night, hat in hand, and said there had been a tragedy. Young William had gotten into a fight at the Elkhorn Saloon and killed a man, knifed him to death in the alley.

"Will may have fought a man," her father said. "That's his nature. But killing a man isn't, unless it was self-defense."

"Witnesses called it murder."

His fist sounded like a gunshot. Alice jumped, then saw where her father had punched a hole in the sluice box. "Murder!" he railed. "My sons are not murderers, Mr. Lobenstein. We'll prove this at William's trial. Where is he being held?"

Mr. Lobenstein didn't answer. His bowler trembled in his hands, and his head bowed further.

"Oh, no," Alice said, knowing.

"Where is my son?" her father boomed.

Still nothing.

"*Where?*"

The merchant finally looked up and tried to answer, but the words became incoherent mumblings, maybe some Hebrew prayer. Her father's long legs carried him quickly across the camp, and he jerked Mr. Lobenstein and shook him like a small rug.

"The vigilantes hanged him, sir!" the merchant cried out. "I'm so terribly sorry, Mr. McKown."

He lowered the little man numbly and stepped back. Lobenstein continued: "I-I-I wanted you to know. D-didn't want you to find out from the v-vigi-vigilantes."

Conall and James stared in shock. Their father slumped to the ground, and Alice ran to him, hugging him tightly as he rocked back and forth, cursing and screaming, "Major Howard's killed my son! That Yankee zealot's killed my son!"

Major Judd Howard was the law in the Moreno Valley. A one-armed man who still carried his rank from the Union Army, Howard had been among the first to arrive in the valley after gold had been discovered and had been among the first to strike it rich. Not from toiling in the gold mines or panning the mountain streams, though. Even before Elizabethtown was laid out, Howard began building saloons, dance halls and gambling parlors. He brought in prostitutes, whiskey peddlers and tinhorns, and soon began buying out other saloon keepers. The nearest civilian law could be found in Santa Fe, too far for justice, so a miner's court was established, and Howard became the head of it that first summer. If a man was charged with a crime—claim jumping, cheating at cards, robbery or even murder—the defendant was brought to Howard's Union Saloon and court members were picked from the establishment's patrons. After testimony, a jury of miners would reach a verdict and Major Howard would pass sentence.

That went on until this January, when Colfax County was created and Elizabethtown became the county seat. You couldn't have a miner's court in a boom town, folks said, so E-Town's populace of transients and permanent residents elected a town marshal. Only a short time thereafter he was identified in a stagecoach robbery as the man who killed the messenger, so Major Howard formed a vigilante group, tracked down the fleeing Marshal Smith and killed him outside of Cimarron. The major, now duly elected mayor, appointed a new marshal and county sheriff, both positions filled by a man named Stevens, who did more than collect taxes and rid the streets of dead animals. King Stevens and the Moreno Valley Vigilante Committee, headed by Mayor Major Howard, handled all of the law enforcement.

They called it law enforcement. Alice's father called it extortion.

And now Major Howard and his vigilantes had killed young Will, and no one could do anything about it.

"Where are you going?" Alice looked up, saw James heading for their father's tent, Conall staring after him in anger.

"To see that blueprint," James snapped. "I don't have your patience, brother."

"James! Stop!"

Conall's words didn't even slow him down. He disappeared inside the Sibley tent, and Alice added a bigger chunk of wood to the fire and walked to her big brother. She could admit her curiosity, but she never would have gone rooting in Papa's tent.

The two brothers had never looked related. Conall had Papa's red hair and solid build, the type of man who would work all day, clearing fields, sawing logs, putting up rafters, chopping cotton or swinging a pick—and he had done it all, and more—and never complain. His face, neck and hands were darkened, and now he clenched his massive fists so tightly that his knuckles whitened. Yet he said nothing more. In that regard, he had been much like their mother.

James had a slimmer build, with dark hair like Alice. He didn't mind hard work, but he preferred to work on his own and not have Papa telling him what to do. He had always been the self-claimed "black sheep," and no one would argue. He'd tell Papa exactly what he felt, and sometimes the two argued so vehemently, Alice thought they would come to blows.

Will had been a little bit like James, but he had always been Papa's favorite. When James came home in his cups or neglected his chores for a horse race, turkey shoot or card game, Papa remained furious for days. But when it was Will . . . "Boy's just sowing his oats." And maybe there was some truth. James might stay gone for two days. If Will slacked off on his chores, you knew he'd come back soon and work harder to make it up to Papa. Only now he wouldn't ever be coming home.

James swore and opened the canvas flap. "Hurry up," he told his siblings. "Before he gets back. You two won't believe this."

Alice glanced at Conall, who turned around and looked at the hilltop cemetery, although it would be hours before Papa finished filling the grave and walking all the way to camp. He stood and took a few uncertain steps, Alice right behind them. Soon, all three stood in the tent and looked at the blueprint James had unrolled onto a wooden camp table.

Alice moved closer and studied the architectural drawing. A two-story building, a pretty big one, too. Papa had carried blueprint paper, pencils, pens, inkwells and assorted tools with him since they left Camden after the War, but he had never done much carpentry work at all, and absolutely no architectural work.

At the top of the page read:

Elizabethtown Courthouse And Jail

Chapter Four

Judd Howard opened the decanter and poured his morning whiskey before sinking into the leather chair behind the cherrywood desk. The rye burned a path down his throat, and he wondered if he would ever get any good liquor out here on the fringes of Perdition. He had been here almost three years, and still he drank whiskey only slightly more palatable than the swill watered down and spiked with tobacco juice and hot sauce that they served at the Elkhorn, Union, Golden Calf and other establishments he owned and operated.

Some dumb Moache Ute had shown up at Fort Union in the fall of '66 with a pretty rock to show to Captain William Moore, the post sutler, hoping to trade the stone for some winter supplies. The rock contained copper ore, and Moore and some associates told the Indian to lead them to the place where he found the rock and he could have plenty of beads, sugar and blankets. Moore, his partners and the Ute came to the Moreno Valley, and one of them started panning the mountain streams just to pass the time. Only he found color. Gold. Baldy Mountain was full of it.

By the next spring, more than three hundred people had rushed to the valley, and Howard came with them, leaving his brothels and confidence men in Denver for a new stake. He would have panned or mined like anyone else if he could, but his left arm ended just above the elbow and he had found it hard to hold a deep-dish pan or swing a pick.

As more and more people flooded the valley, Captain Moore called a town meeting, and the citizens decided to plot out a town on the valley floor. Captain Moore got the honor of naming the new burg, and he decided to honor his little girl. Elizabethtown, they called it, but it proved to be a mouthful for the miners, and they shortened it to E-Town.

Elizabethtown grew, and Howard prospered with it. A stage and freight line ran daily to Cimarron, and a toll road went up through Raton Pass and on to Trinidad, Colorado. Sawmills went into operation. Stores, many of them simply covered wagons parked on town lots, opened. A little Frenchman named Lambert opened the Moreno Hotel, and there was talk that a newspaperman would open up a shop sometime this summer. Judd Howard didn't own the hotel or stores, nor did he lease land from men like Lucien Maxwell to operate a sawmill, and he had no interest in newspapers. He catered to another crowd, and enjoyed it.

He had been a major in the Rebellion, stuck on the

frontier with Colorado Volunteers while others his age, and much younger, won glory on the battlefields back east. Then the stupid secessionists tried to invade New Mexico Territory, taking Albuquerque and Santa Fe before Howard and his commanding officer, Colonel John Chivington, the "Fighting Methodist," stopped the march at Glorieta Pass by hitting the supply train and sending the Rebs back to Texas.

It cost Howard dearly, though. A Confederate Minié ball shattered his left forearm. He still remembered a wide-eyed lieutenant pleading with him: "Sir, let me get you to a surgeon!" And Howard's reply: "Let go of my bridle, Mister. I will not leave this battlefield until the Rebs are running." He stayed in the saddle, too, watching through his binoculars, barking orders, until he reeled from the loss of blood and woke up in a tent with a bloody bandage where his arm should have been.

That had ended the War for Judd Howard. He went back to Denver to recover, missing out while the "Fighting Methodist" made some good Indians out of a band of stinking Cheyenne at Sand Creek. A bunch of the Indian lovers back east called the fight a needless massacre of a peaceful band of mostly women and children, but Judd Howard would have given his other arm to have been there, to have been cheered by the Coloradans in Denver, to show off his scalps and gory trophies and tell any stupid Easterner what he thought about their cries of injustice and condemnation of Colonel Chivington.

The title of "major" he still demanded had helped Howard establish himself in E-Town. He outranked Captain Moore, was a hero in New Mexico Territory if not in the States, so the miners and ruffians elected him as head of the miners' court. Next he became head of the vigilante committee, and now they called him "mayor" as well as "major." At first Major Howard had shown his bias in sentencing those convicted at the miners' court. A man who wore the blue might get run out of town on a rail or banned from E-Town, but an unreconstructed Reb would more than likely face a flogging, or worse. Some former Union soldiers who had fallen to thievery and assault might find themselves recruited by Howard. He could use men who knew how to use their fists or Colt's revolvers, but only if they had worn the blue. He would never, ever trust anyone who had worn the gray. Not after what they did to him at Glorieta.

Once Howard became established as mayor, he became less favorable. Zeke Leonard had ridden with Grierson during his raid behind enemy lines, but he had a pretty good claim below Arthur and Company's Discovery Tree, so when Marshal King Stevens brought in Leonard on charges of robbery and Howard's hand-picked jury found the old Federal cavalry sergeant guilty, Howard, now also "Judge," sentenced Leonard to five years at the territorial prison in Santa Fe. Poor old Sergeant Leonard never made it to Santa Fe, though. He tried to escape, and King Stevens cut him down. Meanwhile, the newly formed J. R. Howard and Company took over the late Mr. Leonard's claim.

Yes, thought Major Judd Robert Howard, Elizabethtown mayor and Colfax County judge, this was turning into a mighty sweet deal.

Even if the whiskey was contemptible.

Someone knocked on the door, and Howard shot down his drink and snapped a command. Marshal

King Stevens entered, closing the door behind him. Deep pits scarred Stevens' face, and his pale blue eyes showed no compassion. He was a man of medium height, dressed in stovepipe boots, black broadcloth pants and coat, and one of those flat-crowned, stiff-brimmed Mexican hats, black also. Stevens hooked his thumbs in the tooled gunbelt that holstered a matching set of Navy Colts butt forward on his hips.

Judd Howard had found Stevens in Trinidad about ten jumps ahead of a posse from Kansas. Stevens had served in neither army during the War, but that didn't matter. He could handle himself, and took orders without question—like the time when that oaf of a marshal, Luke Smith, threw out his empty Spencer carbine and stepped from behind a fort of rocks along the Palisades between E-Town and Cimarron. Smith sighed and grinned when he saw Howard leading the posse.

"Major, I am glad to see you, sir," he said.

Howard didn't smile. "You fool," he said, and lambasted Smith's stupidity with a tirade of curses. "You botched that holdup, and killed a messenger."

"Yeah, but—"

"And you let someone identify you."

The Adam's apple bobbed in the center of the dullard's neck. "If you could loan me a good horse, Major," the man pleaded, "I'll light a shuck to Mexico. Disappear for a while."

Howard shook his head and laughed, but there was no merriment in his voice or face. "You? You couldn't even make it to Cimarron, Smith. You'd never get to Mexico, and then you'd spill your guts."

"No, sir, Major, not me."

King Stevens sat next to Howard on a blue roan

gelding. "Mr. Stevens," Howard said, "how would you handle a situation like this?"

Stevens jerked one of the ivory-handled Colts and fired twice. While the other posse members fought to control their mounts, Howard and Stevens sat calmly, their own horses trained not to flinch at the sound of gunfire. Stevens slid the .36-caliber revolver into the holster and said, "Like that, Major."

Howard smiled, staring at the dead body of Luke Smith, and knew he had found his new marshal.

"What is it?" Howard now asked the dark-haired marshal.

"It's that McKown gent."

"Which one?"

Judd Howard knew the McKowns, strong-willed Southern trash working a claim at one of the creeks between E-Town and Baldy Town. Kept to themselves mostly, as secesh were prone to do, and not one of the lot interested him except that big Scotch-Irish patri-arch's plain-looking daughter, who, with some rouge and a better wardrobe, would fit in well at the Golden Calf or one of the cribs.

"The daddy," Stevens said. "He just bought the last lot on the edge of town from Captain Moore."

"So?"

"I just figured that clan would light a shuck out of here after what happened to their boy, sell the claim and we'd be rid of 'em."

Howard didn't know where this conversation was going. From what he had heard, the McKown claim didn't produce much paydirt, although they must have panned enough if he bought a town lot from Moore. He remembered the youngest McKown boy, or at least what Stevens had told him. Deke Goss, that killer

Beale and the half-breed Gideon had been relieving some lucky gent of his poke, blood and a pound of flesh behind the Elkhorn a few nights back when the kid stuck his big nose into something that wasn't his affair. Thought he was a hero, or some other fool notion. The boy didn't stand a chance against Beale's fists.

Still, he might have recognized Deke Goss, and it wouldn't look right to have one of King Stevens' deputies accused of assault and robbery. So Gideon ended the unconscious gent's lucky streak with his folding knife, and Goss and Beale dragged the bloodied McKown boy to Stevens' office. They came up with the story that McKown had knifed a traveler behind the Elkhorn and fled, only to be caught and hanged on the spot by the vigilantes.

Serious crimes committed at night seldom resulted in trials. Summary justice was more to E-Town's liking, and few citizens complained.

Ian McKown had sworn up and down Front Street that his son had been innocent, but no one listened, and the family, from one of the Carolinas, Alabama or some other Reconstruction-ruled state, held a private ceremony, and that was that. End of story. The McKowns could remain in E-Town or leave. It made no nevermind to Howard, although the McKowns being Southern, he would prefer it if they left. Still, six thousand people now lived in the Moreno Valley, and a lot of those were Rebs. A man couldn't get rid of them all.

"I can't own all of the town lots, Stevens," Howard told the marshal. "And if I wanted that one, I could have bought it a long time ago."

Stevens nodded. "Yes sir, but I thought you should know. Them McKowns . . . they might be trouble."

Howard dismissed that idea with a wave of his hand. He rose from his chair and refilled his shot glass, not offering the marshal any. If Ian McKown wanted to raise Cain, the cemetery could hold him as well as his other sons, even that daughter of his. He returned to his desk and stared at the killer with a badge.

"Anything else?"

"Couple of gamblers rode in late last evening. Checked in at the Moreno and were looking around to set up a table somewhere."

This interested Howard more than some Southerner buying a lot to build a store or something.

"Looking to deal for the house?" he asked. He could always use good dealers. His best faro dealer at the Elkhorn got himself shot to death two months back, and Howard hadn't found a replacement.

"Don't think so, Major. Besides, one's a Texan, big fella, and the other I think fought with the Rebs."

Howard shrugged. He could overlook a gambler's past transgressions if he knew how to win and keep his mouth shut. "Well, I'd best visit these young entrepreneurs and let them know the rules regarding independent gamblers here in E-Town."

"Yes, sir."

"Anything else?"

"That about covers it, Major."

Howard dismissed Stevens with a nod, picked up his glass and sipped the rotgut before he realized something he had forgotten to ask. He called out Stevens' name, and the shootist turned, holding the door partway open, pale eyes waiting.

"What does McKown plan on building on that lot?"

"I don't know, sir," Stevens answered. "But I reckon we'll find out shortly."

Chapter Five

"**Y**ou did what?"

James McKown, unable to control his rage, glared at his father. Arguments came frequently between the two since James had turned twelve years old. Thirteen years later, their disagreements had increased in size and scope. Old Iron-Headed Ian had never liked the way James did anything, from shoeing a horse to shooting a gun, and especially on a construction site. "Scrub those bricks, son. *Harder!*" "You won't hurt that nail, boy. *Hit it!*" "Forget it, James. Let Conall do it." When war broke out, Ian insisted that James and Will stay behind to protect their mother and sister while Old Ian and Conall enlisted in Kershaw's Brigade and marched off to fight the Yankee tyrants. James disobeyed his dad once more, though, joining up with Palmetto State's Fourth Infantry and letting thirteen-year-old Will be the man of the house.

Of course, when James, his father and older brother returned to Camden after Appomattox, their house had been burned—not from Sherman's troops but from a bolt of lightning—and Will had been conscripted when he turned sixteen and wound up fighting in the Army of the Tennessee, where he was captured at Franklin and no one knew if he was still alive. Will showed up two months later, weak but alive, and Mama had taken consumption. Old Iron-Headed Ian blamed James for that, too.

The doctors said Mama would do better out West, so the McKowns packed up and headed to Texas. They left too late for Mama, though, and wound up burying her in Natchitoches, Louisiana. James should have left right after that, maybe made his way back to Natchez, Mississippi, to try his hand at cards or perhaps to New Orleans. He had heard a lot about that town and had never seen a big city unless you counted Columbia or Richmond, and neither of those looked like much by '65. But Will talked him into staying, saying the family had to stick together now that Mama was gone. So, Will followed Papa and his siblings on to Texas, finding some work in Jefferson and Dallas but never staying in one place too long.

Old Iron-Headed Ian had become restless—shiftless might be a better word for it—after the war. Always looking for something new, to "see the elephant," he called it. Back in the war, that had meant to experience battle; now it meant to find out what was beyond the next ridge. When the Texans started herding those ornery longhorns to the railheads in Kansas, the McKowns traveled north, working in Abilene. A body could find plenty of work in the cowtowns, and Papa started saving a lot of Yankee greenbacks, yellow-backs and hard money in that tin box he hid underneath the seat of their wagon. But then shiftless Ian heard about the gold fields in northern New Mexico Territory. They became miners. Did all right, too, although Will and James lost a good deal of their piddling allowance to the sharks and strumpets that filled E-Town at night.

And now Old Iron-Headed Ian said he had bought a lot in town to build a memorial to Will. That courthouse and jail he had dreamed up after Will got himself hanged by the vigilantes. Papa never touched liquor, but he sure sounded as if he had a belly full of swamp tonic. Dumb Conall nodded his big head, liking the idea of building a courthouse. Alice just stared at the fire, probably thinking of that tinhorn she was wooing and trying to keep Papa from finding out.

"If you want to build a memorial to Will," James found himself saying, "build a saloon." He shook his head and swore underneath his breath. "How do you expect to make any money off a courthouse?" And he cursed again.

"It's not about money," McKown thundered. "It's about William, and I won't have you blaspheming his name."

"What about supplies?" asked Conall, ever the peacekeeper, always the man of reason.

"We'll get lumber from the sawmills. I've already sent an order in for more equipment, tools and such that we don't have. We'll have to hire some more workers, but I think we can have the building completed before the first snow. It'll be mighty fine."

"Why?" James was flabbergasted. "What's the point? It won't bring Will back."

"No," he said. "But it's the first step to bringing some semblance of law to this Gomorrah. And I think your younger brother would understand. This is for him."

James kept the next vehement oath to himself. This stupid jail didn't have anything to do with Will. It was all about Papa, Old Iron-Headed Ian at it again. There was no profit in this. If the people of E-Town wanted a courthouse, they would ask the civic leaders to put one up. And Major Howard definitely would not allow real law, real justice to come to this flop-house and tent city until he had bled the valley dry.

"When do you want to start?" Conall asked.

"I figured we can get to work digging the foundation tomorrow morning. The three of us can do that easily enough. We'll move to town, work there. I'll hire help, and when the supplies arrive we can start putting up the frame."

Foundation? Papa was loco. You didn't build a house on a pier and beam foundation in this country. You lay wide planks on the ground, if you bothered at all. A sod floor seemed good enough for most folks. And why slave away to put up a frame building? Log cabins would be a whole lot easier, and probably a good deal warmer. Old Iron-Headed Ian thought he was back on the Wateree River, putting up some showoff home for a cotton or tobacco planter. Miners and the parasites who swarmed to gold camps didn't need much in the ways of comfort, and they certainly didn't need a courthouse and jail.

"Sounds good to me," Conall said.

James knew he couldn't check his temper. "Well, it

doesn't sound good to me," he blurted out. "Where do you think you'll get the money to build this memorial, Papa? Tell me that. You think Captain Moore is gonna offer you a tidy sum—or maybe Major Howard?"

"I won't take money from Captain Moore," he answered, deliberately omitting Howard. "I won't take money from anyone. This is for Will. It's our gift in his honor."

James shook his head. "You still haven't answered my question. Nails and wood cost money, not to mention doors and iron bars. This is a jail, remember? And shipping that stuff from Santa Fe or more than likely somewhere back in Missouri? Yankee merchants won't be interested in making donations in Will's honor. You haven't saved *that* much money."

"The money will come. God will see to that. And we will work, starting tomorrow. I've had enough of this conversation."

He turned for his tent, but stopped when James angrily shouted: "I won't be a part of this poppycock. If you and Conall want to build this jail, go ahead. But I won't be laughed at as a fool—which is what you are, Papa."

There. He had said it. Cut the cord. Will wasn't here to talk him out of it this time. He had finally broken the ties, although it looked like he might have to fight his way out of this one. Papa stormed toward him, fists clenched, face flushing in anger. James took a couple of uncontrollable steps back, got ready to dodge those staggering blows he knew Old Iron-Headed Ian could deliver.

Conall's voice stopped his father. "He's right, Father."

That surprised both James and stubborn Papa. Both

men looked at Conall, who said evenly: "We don't need James's help, Father. He never was much of a carpenter anyway. And we'll need money, need someone to work our claim. James can do that."

"Right." Sarcasm filled James's voice. "I break my back panning for gold while the two of you spend all of the money on some courthouse no one in the valley wants. If you think—"

"Shut up, James!"

James turned to his sister, surprised that she had even been listening to the argument, shocked at the anger in her voice. Alice stood. She reminded him of his mother, furious, trying not to tremble with outrage when he had told her he was joining up to fight the Yanks. At first he thought Alice might cry, but he soon saw the grit in her face. McKowns didn't cry. She may have looked like Mama, but inside she was just like Old Iron-Headed Ian.

"That's the least you can do, brother," Alice told him. "And I'm sure we won't take all of your money. There'll be some left over for you to give to the crib girls." She kicked at the fire and turned quickly, storming her way out of camp, heading for town, probably to visit that Yankee chiseler she thought she was seeing secretly. He wondered if she would cry on his shoulder.

Outnumbered, James relented. "All right," he told his father and brother, although his eyes never left Alice's back as she marched away. "As long as I don't have to take part in your scheme, I'll stay here and work the claim."

"Good," his father said. "Conall and I don't need your help."

* * *

It felt good, Catherine Alice McKown thought, to put the stupid family squabbles behind her. Let James and Papa fight it out among themselves while Conall stood like a clod and watched. There were times like today when she really hated Hugh Morris. Hugh came from a good family who had a fine plantation on the Little Lynches River in Kershaw County. The Morris family went back several generations in South Carolina, and Hugh's great-great-grandfather had fought with General Thomas Sumter, "The Gamecock," during the Revolution. Educated at The Citadel down in Charleston, charming, intelligent and ever the gentleman, a man who raised thoroughbreds that could outrun the wind and had even been to Paris and London, Hugh had to be one of the most eligible bachelors in both Carolinas. Coquettes and real ladies practically threw themselves on him—he could have picked anyone between Savannah and Richmond—but Hubert Longley Saint John Morris chose the sixteen-year-old daughter of a Camden carpenter and sometime architect, and Alice pledged herself to Hugh.

Then came the war, and with his military training at The Citadel, Hugh earned a commission as captain and went off to fight, carrying a lock of Alice's hair with him as he rode off with the promise that they would be wed as soon as the abolitionists and Union despots were licked. So Alice waited. And the gallant Hubert Longley Saint John Morris, now a lieutenant colonel, fell at a place in Pennsylvania called Gettysburg.

If the fire-eaters on both sides, North and South, had tried to work things out peacefully, if men weren't men, then she would now be Mrs. Hubert Longley Saint John Morris, no longer able to hear the habitual shouting matches between Papa and James. Even Will would probably still be alive, and the McKowns and Morrises would be in South Carolina, sipping mint julep tea and fanning themselves on the veranda—not eking out an existence in this beautiful, yet harsh and cold, place they called New Mexico.

Mama said she would find another, but for a long time Alice didn't want to think about another man in her life. She had had a few suitors, a farmer's son in South Carolina, and a cobbler in Dallas, but Alice did her best to dissuade them, or dismiss them when they became persistent. Mama told her she was just as stubborn as Papa when she turned down the last proposal from the farmer, a boy named Ezra Gregory, and maybe Mama had been right. But she didn't love Ezra, and she certainly didn't love the Texas cobbler with his crooked teeth, Ichabod Crane nose and bad manners. Even Mama, had she lived, would not have wanted the cobbler for a son-in-law. So brokenhearted Alice traveled with Papa and her brothers from place to place, cooking, sewing, cleaning . . . Will had teased her that she was doomed to a life as a scullery maid for Papa and her brothers.

She was twenty-four years old now. The girls she went to school and church with back in Camden were raising families, while she was basically a servant for the McKowns, well on her way to becoming an old maid. Will had been right. But now, in this brutal frontier settlement called Elizabethtown, Alice had met someone new, someone who almost made her forget about her plain face and calloused hands, her shabby clothes and forgotten manners, even Hugh Morris.

Jeffrey Rowley had fair skin and sparkling blue eyes, a quick wit and tender hands. He dealt for the house at the Elkhorn Saloon, had admittedly served under General Grant, and rode with the Moreno Valley Vigilante Committee, all of which would doom the kind Ohioan in Papa's stubborn mind. But he treated her kindly, and she liked the way he held her and, wickedly, even enjoyed the taste of whiskey and tobacco when they kissed.

They met behind the Montezuma Bar and Clubs Rooms, one of the few gambling halls that Major Howard didn't own. Jeff told her she shouldn't come to town after dark alone, but she informed him that she had been taking care of herself for years. He laughed, and stopped worrying.

He crushed out a cigarette when he saw her and ran, like a schoolboy, to her. She liked that, too. They embraced, kissed and ducked into an alley out of view from the passers-by that streamed down the streets night and day.

"Alice," he said. "I'm so sorry about your brother. I want you to know that I had nothing to do with that. If I had, I swear to you that I would have stopped them from hanging him. I wanted to go to the funeral, to pay my respects—"

She pressed her fingers against his lips, knowing, understanding. She didn't want to talk about Will anymore.

"You're not pulling out, are you?" he asked, his voice pleading.

"No. Papa's staying. And if he left, I think I would stay."

They kissed briefly. He pulled away, holding her and smiling. "I hear your father bought a town lot. Are you leaving your claim?"

She shook her head. "You won't believe it, Jeff. I don't believe it myself."

Chapter Six

E-Town, Frank Ivy declared, would make Abilene's
"Devil's Addition" look like a gathering of blue-haired
quilters back in the Shenandoah. He and Sam Raintree
had split up shortly after arriving here, roaming from
gambling parlor to gambling den in search of a likely
place to set up a table and relieve some miners of their
pokes. He had yet to find anything he liked, but passed
a few hours at the Crazy Ute by sitting in at a poker
game and breaking even, maybe winning a couple of
bucks. The Crazy Ute was nothing more than a few
tarps and bearskins hanging from a frame of pine logs
and two-by-fours, with uncomfortable chairs, warped
tables, and a sod floor that left the soles of his boots
thick with mud. The barkeep dispensed whiskey
straight from a keg, and the whole establishment—if

you could call it that—smelled of sour sweat, rancid mud and stale tobacco smoke.

Yet the Crazy Ute was packed with people, few of whom seemed to mind (or were too drunk to notice) that the house dealers were obvious cheaters and the scantily clad harlots who tried to coax customers into buying them a drink or partaking in other refreshments also signaled the dealers what their "escorts" held.

The clean air felt good, and Ivy crossed the muddy street to try the Elkhorn Saloon. At least it had real walls, maybe even a real floor, and if he couldn't find a table, perhaps a beer would wash down the taste of the forty-rod scamper juice he had sipped at the Crazy Ute. Frank put his right hand on the top of the batwing door and hesitated. For some reason, he had a bad feeling about this place.

"Evening," a voice said.

Frank turned, and stepped back from the door. His eyes took in the man leaning against one of the two pine columns that held a makeshift awning over the Elkhorn's entrance. An ugly man, with a pockmarked face and uncaring, unforgiving eyes, dressed in black and wearing a brace of Navy Colts and a five-point tin star stamped MARSHAL.

"I'm also Colfax County sheriff," the lawman said, "but I like 'marshal' better."

Ivy nodded. Lawmen and gamblers usually had a tenuous relationship, and Frank didn't like the look of this gent. He waited for the marshal to make his point.

"The major wants to see you."

"Major?"

"Major Howard," the marshal said, and added, "Major Judd Howard," as if the name carried weight here. And it must have, but Frank hadn't been in town more than twenty-four hours. The marshal slightly tilted his head in the direction of the Elkhorn. "He's inside. Let's go."

"Understand you're looking to set up an honest game," Howard said in his upstairs office above the Elkhorn's gaming rooms. The major spoke soberly, but Frank quickly noticed the bloodshot eyes and smelled the whiskey on Howard's breath. They had shaken hands after introducing themselves, and Frank regretted his gaze lasting a second too long on the major's missing arm. Howard didn't care much for that, Ivy could tell, but he dismissed it and forced a smile.

Howard offered Frank a drink, and he accepted. He didn't really want a whiskey but nor did he want to offend the major after his earlier faux pas. Besides, Judd Howard probably had pretty good stock up here in his private office. The major filled a couple of tumblers and handed one to Frank. They held their glasses up in a silent toast, and Ivy took a sip. Well, he thought as the coal oil burst into flames and roared down his throat, it was a hair better than the snake-head poured at the Crazy Ute.

"I own and operate the bulk of the gambling dens and saloons in E-Town," Howard said, placing his already empty tumbler on his desktop. "Can always use a good man."

Ivy smiled. "Thanks, Mr. Howard—"

"It's *Major* Howard."

The smile disappeared. Howard seemed to hear the sorry-not-interested tone in Ivy's voice. "Major," Frank corrected. "I've never been comfortable playing with other folks' money," he said, trying to sound polite. "I've never been interested in dealing for the house."

Howard nodded. "I understand. I detect a Southern accent, sir. Tennessee?"

"Virginia," he answered reluctantly. Asking a man's name or his home was considered downright unsociable on the frontier. If a man wanted you to know where he came from, he'd tell you.

"You fought in the late Rebellion?"

Frank slid his half-finished drink onto Howard's table. "I fought in the War for Southern Independence, sir." He had lost his apologetic tone, and wanted to get out of Howard's office as soon as possible.

"You lost," the major said, and laughed abruptly. "It doesn't matter, Ivy. I just like to know a man's background, especially if he plans on doing business in my town."

My town. Frank began to think he should have stayed in Cimarron.

"Anyway, there are plenty of tables for rent if you'd care to set up a game," Howard went on. "But you need to know the rules. The house in any of my gaming halls takes fifteen percent of your winnings. That's on top of fifty dollars a night for the table."

"Seems high," Ivy said evenly. An understatement. It was brazen robbery.

"It is, Ivy. I'll admit that. But the fifty a night covers us in case you're unlucky and lose and we can't take our fifteen percent. Secondly, and most importantly, this is Elizabethtown, New Mexico Territory, not Richmond, Virginia. The fifteen percent we take, as well as the fifty a night, that is for your own good."

"How's that?"

The marshal answered. "Protection." Frank turned

in his chair, saw the pockmarked man leaning against the door, smiling mirthlessly. Ivy thought the man had left the room after introducing him to Howard. He was a quiet one, catlike. Ivy knew he would do well to remember that.

"Marshal Stevens is right," Howard said, and Frank faced the major once more. "E-Town has a violent element, Ivy. If you win, without our protection, you might find it hard to keep your winnings. There's no bank here."

"I'm sure Marshal Stevens does a fine job keeping the peace," Ivy said, his voice laced with derision.

"He does. So does our vigilante committee. But our cemetery on the hilltop overlooking town is full of unlucky gamblers."

Frank ignored the veiled threat. "This protection fee," he said. "Is it required at all of the gambling halls in E-Town, or just the ones you own?"

The major's bloodshot eyes hardened. "You're free to look around, free to try your luck as a licensed gambler at another establishment, or to sit in at any of our honest tables. Think it over, Ivy."

Honest tables. The roulette wheels were rigged. Frank had spotted that in minutes. So were the faro layouts, and he would bet his McInerney boots that the cards supplied at the Elkhorn or any other of Howard's dens were marked. Ivy rose, nodded curtly at the major and walked away without thanking Howard for the drink, or free advice.

Marshal Stevens blocked the door, his thumbs hooked in his gunbelt near the matching pair of Colts.

Lawman? Frank had been generous. This ruffian was nothing more than a hired killer. Ivy stopped, waiting, not saying a word. A gambler knew to pick and choose his fights, and he didn't want this to be one of them. Frank was no match for a shootist like this Stevens, and he didn't want to be buried on that windswept hill before he turned thirty-two with only Sam Raintree to mourn his untimely passing. Yet, facing a killer or not, Frank wasn't going to cower in front of Stevens, and he certainly wouldn't politely ask him to step aside. Southern pride. It had killed a lot of men. It would probably kill him one day.

Someone knocked on the door, and Frank felt the tension ease. Stevens unhooked his left hand and found the doorknob. His right hand moved deliberately until it rested on the ivory handle of one of the pistols. Then, with an uneasy smile and those cold eyes that never left Ivy, the killer stepped aside and pulled open the door.

Ivy saw a young man standing in the upstairs hallway, high-crowned black hat in his slender hands. Blue trousers with red and white stripes were stuck in the tops of his black cavalry-style boots, and a red gabardine vest with rounded lapel, white shirt with paper collar and blue narrow necktie completed his outfit. That and the percussion-capped derringer sticking out of his vest pocket.

"Excuse me," the young man said as he brushed past Ivy.

"What did you find out, Rowley?" he heard the major ask as Stevens slammed the door.

Sam Raintree smiled over supper in the Moreno Hotel's dining room. "So that Yankee carpetbagger held a polite interview with yourself, too? What did you tell 'm?"

"That I wasn't interested. Found a less expensive table at the Montezuma."

"Yeah. That gyp's take of fifteen percent and fifty a night would mean a fella would have to cheat to make any profit. Wonder how much he pays his dealers."

"You plan on working for him?"

"Not yet. Told him I'd think about it. He and that tinhorn shootist of his didn't like that much. 'Sides, I don't think he cared much for my Texas heritage, that Yankee scamp. Anyhow, I ain't rightly figured out what I'll do next. Thought I might ride up to Baldy Town, see if I can skin some miners there. Or I could see if I can best those cheatin' swine at the Crazy Ute or Elkhorn. I fancy myself a pretty good cheater when I'm a mind to."

"I wouldn't try that, Sam," Ivy said, stopping his mug of coffee just below his lips. The Texan smiled at Ivy's concern.

"Don't you go worryin' over my hide, Frank. I ain't leavin' this valley till I've got a good stake to set me up down south somewheres this winter. And you know me. I ain't one who needs to cheat at cards to win. I'll find a game somewhere. 'Sides, it was my idea to come here, remember?"

Frank tested the coffee. "Baldy Town, huh?"

Baldy Town lay almost all the way up Baldy Mountain, supplying the workers at Lucien Maxwell's Aztec and Montezuma mines with a place to blow off steam and spend their hard-earned money. It lacked the crowds of E-Town, but in all likelihood it also lay beyond the reach of Major Judd Howard's stranglehold. Frank wanted to plant the seed of Baldy Town again. He enjoyed Raintree's company, but he didn't want the Texan to tangle with that killer Stevens. And if Raintree stayed in E-Town, he and Stevens would fight. As well as Frank knew Sam Raintree, that was an even-money bet.

"Might be somethin' there, Frank," the Texan said. "You work E-Town, I work Baldy Town, and I bet in a month we'll have to rent a freight wagon to haul out our winnin's. You think you can stay out of trouble if I mosey on up that mountain."

"I'll try," Frank said, not showing his relief.

Ivy's gaze swept pass the Texan and focused on the burly redheaded man suddenly standing in the doorway. Muscles bulged underneath the dirty homespun shirt, and a pair of stained canvas suspenders held up his denim trousers. He shifted his feet nervously, drawing Ivy's attention to the scuffed brogans. His mouth opened and closed, and a Mexican waiter asked if he'd care to be seated. The towering man shook his head. Maybe he couldn't afford a meal, Frank thought. The newcomer carried no weapon, unless you counted those thick hands, and stared into the crowd of patrons.

"Folks," he finally said, and now Raintree slid around in his chair to watch the newcomer. The patter of dining-room conversation and scratching of utensils against tin plates stopped. The stranger suddenly looked old, maybe sixty—it was hard to tell. His clothing and weathered brow bespoke of a hard life, yet he still carried himself with pride.

"Hate to interrupt your supper, but I got an mighty important announcement. I'm looking for carpenters, experienced ones if they can be had, but I'll take anyone with a strong back and willingness to learn. I'll pay thirty cents a day and three square meals a day, no work on the Sabbath." That brought a few snickers in the dining hall. Even a hermit would find it hard to live in a place as expensive as E-Town on eight dollars a month. The man continued, pretending he hadn't heard the chortling. Proud, Ivy thought.

"Anyway. If you're interested, the name's Mc-Kown. Ian McKown. I'll be putting up a building on the east side of town, me and my son. Starting tomorrow. And if you know someone who needs the work, I can use a man who ain't scared of hammers and nails. Thank you, folks. Mighty sorry to bust in on your supper."

He left, head high and back straight. Sam Raintree grinned as he swung around to face Ivy.

"Well," the Texan said. "Lucky for you, bein' an old carpenter and all." He snorted, unable to control his laughter. "Iffen you get cleaned out at the poker tables, I bet you can find work with that old man."

Ivy shook his head. "Not hardly, Sam," he said.

Chapter Seven

Major Judd Howard had waited too long. He should have done something quickly about that stupid Southerner's dream of building a courthouse and jail in E-Town, put that fire out before it got too hot. By thunder, a visiting reporter from the *Santa Fe New Mexican* had already written a short article about the secessionist McKown, and the carpenter had plenty of help these days, hammering and sawing. The foundation had been laid, and wooden frames began making McKown's dream seem more like an actual building.

The Elizabethtown Courthouse and Jail.

Howard had a pretty good belly laugh over that with King Stevens. "You should go over there and thank the old man," Howard said as soon as that monte sharp Rowley informed them of McKown's plans. "He's building you a new office. Although I'm not sure about needing a jail. When have you ever brought in a prisoner alive, King?"

Stevens had laughed at that, too, but the gambler Rowley didn't see much humor in that. Maybe he was really sweet on that carpenter's girl, and didn't like being asked—well, *asked* might not have been the correct word—to use that petticoat for information. Not that Judd Howard cared one way or the other.

"I wouldn't take this courthouse thing too lightly, Major," Rowley said.

"How's that?" Howard wiped his eyes and reached for the decanter of whiskey.

"If McKown gets that courthouse built, you'll be out of luck. A real judge might be next, and your vigilante committee would find itself out of favor in the valley. Who knows? E-Town might decide to get itself a real marshal, too."

Guts. Howard had to give Rowley a little credit, speaking that way to King Stevens. The marshal only scoffed and said, "McKown will never get that jail finished."

"I don't know," Rowley said. "He's mighty stubborn."

Two weeks had passed, and as Judd Howard sat in his office with three whiskeys already warming his body, he realized Jeff Rowley had been right. That fool McKown had drummed up a lot of support. Men like Captain Moore, Henry Lambert and Joel Lobenstein, known as the "pillars of the community" by the less rowdy residents of E-Town but merely cretins and nuisances to Judd Howard, were singing the praises of Ian McKown. Just last night Howard heard someone say, "Buildin' that courthouse will be the first step to riddin' the valley of undesirables."

Maybe they thought of Major Judd Howard, the town's mayor, by thunder, as one of those "undesirables."

Just thinking about it made Howard boil. Fuming, he shot up and jerked open the top drawer of his desk. He grabbed the Whitney-Beals .28-caliber Walking Beam, checked the percussion caps, and shoved the revolver into his coat pocket. It was time, he decided, to pay Ian McKown a belated visit.

The three hired hands wolfed down the sandwiches Alice had made like starving coyotes. Well, Ian McKown thought, he had worked them pretty hard. A Mexican named Griego, a burly black man called T. J. and a civilized Ute who answered to Shem. Not the best crew McKown had ever worked, but they earned their thirty cents a day. He and Conall saw to that. Fact was, though, that he was mighty proud of those boys.

The building was ahead of schedule. Pretty soon, he'd have to stop construction until the rest of the supplies arrived. Conall handed him a sandwich and canteen, and Ian found a place in the shade. His lungs worked hard—he had never quite gotten accustomed to the thin air in these mountains—and he felt twinges of pain in his right arm, his legs ached, and pain shot up and down his back. He had worn himself out, too.

He ate the sandwich without really tasting it, and sipped on the canteen, neither hungry nor thirsty. Just tired. And feeling old. In just a couple of weeks, on July 4 to be exact, he would turn sixty years old. He had never really thought of himself as an old man, but the past nine years had been tough. Four years of war, and he still carried a Yankee ball in his left shoulder from Manassas. Then coming home to a ruined home and almost wrecked family. Heading west, trying to make a new life, and the cost of his foolish dreams. A wife buried in Louisiana, and his youngest son here in New Mexico. One son who probably hated him, and a daughter he couldn't understand. At least there was Conall, the oldest, thirty years old now and a good man. A better carpenter than even himself.

"Father, we got a visitor."

Ian corked the canteen, and looked at Conall, seeing a reflection of himself from thirty years ago. His oldest boy jerked his head toward the main road, and McKown struggled to rise, more exhausted than he had first thought. Once he could outwork any man, and now just standing up left him out of breath. He waited a few seconds before walking past Conall. Visitors were frequent at the construction site. Captain Moore's family sometimes brought them food and wished them luck, and the merchant Lobenstein would deliver nails and other supplies. There had been the reporter from down in Santa Fe, and other visitors, most idlers and ne'er-do-wells with nothing better to do, even that shootist called Clay Allison, but a lot of good folks, also: a Methodist circuit rider named Dyer, a family of settlers down near Black Lake and a fellow known as Uncle Dick Wootton, who had built the road that ran northeast through Raton Pass and into Colorado Territory.

McKown stopped abruptly when he saw Major Howard leaning against their wagon, talking idly to the hired carpenters. He wore a brown high derby with tan binding and band and a dark plaid sack coat with the left sleeve pinned up above his elbow and the hammer of a small revolver sticking out from a pocket.

"Hello, McKown. First of all, I should apologize for neglecting my duties as town mayor. I should have been here much sooner, but you know how work goes," Howard said easily, although the smile was forced. He held out his right hand, which Ian ignored. The major's grin disappeared and he lowered his arm.

"What do you want?" His men had stopped eating, aware of the edge in his voice. T. J. rose and walked to Conall, ready to busy himself somewhere else. Shem and Griego watched in silence.

"Trying to be neighborly, McKown," Howard said, nodding at the building behind him. "Looks like it's coming right along."

"It is."

"Good. No, I should say excellent. We need a courthouse. We need a jail. As much as Marshal Stevens and the Vigilante Committee strive to keep the peace in the Moreno Valley, it's a hard job, almost impossible. We need to bring peace to E-Town, to make this city a good home for families such as yourself. We need to eliminate the robberies and murders—"

"Like the murder of my son, William."

Howard stopped. His mouth moved, but no words came forth, and his face went blank. The wretch had forgotten all about William. The major took another breath and, after recovering, said, "My condolences, sir, for your tragic loss. Yes, that's what I mean. And once this courthouse is completed, Marshal Stevens will have a fine office to uphold the peace and law." He forced a laugh. "Perhaps even I shall move in from my cramped quarters above the Elkhorn. After all, I am mayor."

McKown spoke with forced control. "The only way you or that killer Stevens will ever set foot inside this building is if you are both in shackles, sir."

Judd Howard's ears reddened. "Now, see here, McKown—"

But Ian cut him off. "Get off my property, Howard. You're nothing more than a carpetbagger and a plunderer. If I could prove that you had anything to do with William's death, I'd string you up myself—"

"McKown, I'm the duly elected mayor, you insolent son of—"

Ian's resounding oath stopped the mayor like a hammer. "You," McKown said tightly, "are a pathetic little drunkard, a coward who hires killers like that Stevens to do your dirty work. They tell me that a Rebel ball took off your arm at Glorieta, but I think it also severed the humanity in you, if you ever had any. You still hate the South, still blame those of us who wore the gray for your arm, but that's just an excuse. You'd cut your own mother's throat if you saw a profit in it. I've asked you to leave my property, Howard. Do so now, or they'll carry you out of here."

The slamming door sounded like a cannon shot, and the concussion knocked the elkhorn nailed above the window to crash onto the floor. Judd Howard didn't care. He swore savagely as he crossed his office, kicked the cherry-wood desk with his mule-ear boots and reached for the decanter. Empty. He swore again, flinging the glass against the wall where it shattered. His hand gripped the walnut butt of the revolver, and he ripped his coat jerking the Walking Beam. His finger slipped inside the trigger ring, and he wondered why he hadn't just killed McKown there.

No one spoke to him like that. No one.

He couldn't have just shot McKown, not with the witnesses. Even as mayor, even owning the vigilantes and most of the town, shooting an unarmed man would be frowned upon by those idiot "pillars of the community." But that stubborn piece of Southern trash would pay dearly for those comments.

Howard slid the iron-frame revolver across the desk and stormed out of his office, leaning on the wooden railing and looking downstairs. "Goss!" he shouted, and the short killer with the green eyes looked up from the bar.

"Yes, Major?" Deke Goss asked.

"Where's Rowley?"

"Went to the privy, sir. Should be back in a minute."

"I want him up here as soon as he's back. Understand?"

"Yes sir."

"And I want you to find King Stevens. Pronto."

Goss shot down his whiskey and sped out the door.

"Hold it. I'm not finished!"

The little man spun around, almost tripping. "Yes, sir?"

"Get the new man up here, too. The brute with the fists."

"The Man-Killer?"

Howard nodded, dismissing the deputy marshal wanted for murder back in the States. "That's right," he said, softly. "Man-Killer Roland Beale."

Chapter Eight

They met behind the Montezuma, embraced and ducked into the alley. Saturday night and payday meant E-Town swarmed with miners already well in their cups and the sun was just beginning to dip behind the mountains. Jeff Rowley pulled back and gazed at her, smiling. "You look lovely tonight, Alice," he said, and kissed her forehead. "Absolutely lovely."

She blushed. Jeff was lying. How could she look lovely when she owned two dresses, one gray wool, one blue and white gingham, and for the past couple of weeks had been clad more in Will's jeans and even one of his shirts, now cooking for not only her big brother and father but three carpenters. This afternoon she had even helped drive nails into the floor planks. Lovely. What would the society girls back in Camden say about her now, wearing a man's clothing—her dead brother's clothes, at that—and doing a man's work.

"I can't stay long," Jeff told her. "I wish I could, but Major Howard will tack my hide to the wall if he finds out I'm here and not fleecing those double-jackers and sluicers. How's the jail coming along?"

"Fine," she said, trying not to hide her disappointment that their rendezvous would be so short.

"Well, maybe we can see each other tomorrow."

She shook her head. "We're going to the claim to see James."

"All of you?"

"Just Conall, Papa and me."

"What about your carpenters?"

She shrugged. "I imagine they'll stay at camp or wander into town to spend their pay."

Jeff laughed. "From what I hear your father's paying, it won't last them long."

He must have seen the hurt in her face, because he pulled her close and hugged her, kissing her hair, and saying warmly, "Oh, dearest, I wish I could go with you tomorrow. I wish you could stay with me tonight." She looked up, and he bent his head and kissed her. "One day," he said when he pulled away, "I'll take you away from here. To San Francisco. Anywhere you want to go, my love."

She tried smiling and pulled away. "I'd better go," she said. "I'll see you Monday?"

"Of course. I'll be here."

"Tomorrow then," the Major told Rowley. "You've done good work." Howard smiled at the gambler.

"Now you'd best go down and do some more good work, win a few thousand for the house."

Jeff Rowley closed the door behind him, and the Major fired up a cigar, not bothering to offer one to that small killer from Missouri or Roland Beale himself.

Beale towered over the man called Goss, Major Howard, even the town marshal—and King Stevens towered over many men. Beale stood silently, away from the others, waiting for the Major to give him his orders and wondering how he came to find himself with such miserable company in a savage town, a long, long way from New York City.

His parents had been slaves, but Roland Beale had been born a freedman and grew up as an apprentice sailmaker in Philadelphia. Of course, he wasn't known as Roland Beale back then. His parents were Margaret and George Wilson, and they named their only son John Adams Wilson. Folks nicknamed him "Mr. President," and he had liked that growing up. But he never really stopped growing up. By the time he turned twelve, he stood over six feet tall in his stockings, and he kept growing until he measured six-feet-six and weighed a powerful two hundred and sixty pounds.

Size didn't intimidate many freedman in Philadelphia, and "Mr. President" found himself in a lot of friendly boxing matches. He never lost, never even got knocked down, and pretty soon he was earning a tidy sum taking all comers, black and white. When he turned twenty-one, he knocked out a boxer from Liverpool named Martin Simon, and when the Englishman woke up, he told John A. Wilson that he was wasting a god-given gift by making sails. He was a boxer—just needed a good manager—so Simon and John "The Giant" Wilson moved to New York.

They did well, Mr. Simon giving good lessons and "The Giant" listening, boxing with his bare fists and besting everyone. And then New York turned crazy in '63. People fighting on the streets, cursing the war and the conscription laws. Young John Wilson had wanted to join one of the Union Army's black regiments, but Mr. Simon wouldn't let him. And now, in the middle of the city, some young Irishman with a bloody nose charged "The Giant" with a broken whiskey bottle, screaming at the top of his lungs that the riot was all this black man's fault. Scared, he dodged the swipe of the ragged bottle, and hit the Irishman hard. The man dropped easily, eyes open, still clutching the bottle.

Mr. Simon knelt to check on the Irishman and looked up, his face ashen. "Johnny," he whispered. "You've killed him, Johnny. You've murdered him."

"I didn't mean to," he cried. "I swear to God I didn't mean to."

They fled. Mr. Simon said they had to, said the coppers would hang them both if they stayed in New York. His name had to go, Mr. Simon, told him in Louisville, Kentucky, snapping his fingers and saying, "Roland Beale. From now on, Johnny, you are Man-Killer Roland Beale."

He hadn't cared much for the name, but six years later it was all he answered to. They boxed in Kentucky, Indiana, Illinois and Minnesota during the war, then worked their way up and down the Mississippi after the South was whipped and the slaves freed. Cairo. Fort Madison. Hannibal. Saint Louis. Vicksburg. Baton Rouge. Memphis. The nickname proved prophetic, too. Man-Killer Roland Beale killed another man in a bare-knuckle prizefight in Prairie du Chien, Wisconsin. Another man never woke up after taking a pounding in Matamoros, Mexico, after Mr. Simon and Man-Killer turned west.

By then, Mr. Simon had developed a new game, taking bets against all comers that no one could remain standing for two rounds against the great Man-Killer Roland Beale. And no one ever did, until some blow-hard Texan with a head like an anvil wobbled and weaved, but never fell, on a winter night in Dallas last year. Martin Simon, who never could pick the horses and spent too much on whiskey and the ladies, couldn't pay off his bets, and the city constable hauled him off to jail and told Roland Beale he'd best get out of town.

He had drifted, trying to find work but landing nothing more than swamping saloons or cleaning liveries, until two rogues jumped him outside a hog ranch near Fort Union. One fell with a broken jaw, and the other dragged himself away with busted ribs and a mangled face. He heard someone strike a match, and turned savagely.

"You want some of it, too, mister?" Beale said with a snarl.

"Not me, friend," the man answered, shaking out the match and taking a long pull on his cigarette. "Fact is, I might have a job for you up in E-Town." He pulled back his coat, revealing the star pinned to his vest, and introduced himself. "The name's King Stevens."

So here he was, three months later, still Man-Killer Roland Beale, falling lower into this cistern, while John A. Wilson, "Mr. President the sailmaker," had become a disjointed dream.

"Beale, Goss," Major Howard said, bringing Man-Killer's attention to the sordid present. "I want you two to get rid of those carpenters, and tear down that building tomorrow."

"Yes, Major," Deke Goss said, and Roland Beale found himself nodding and saying, "Yes, sir," too.

He let Deke Goss do the talking, watching the runt from Missouri boast, right hand always resting on the Army Colt stuck in his waistband. Beale studied the faces of the three carpenters. The black man was a coward. So was the Indian. Maybe not really cowards, but not threats in this situation. The Mexican, however, might put up a fight. If that happened, Goss would either shoot him, or Beale would bash a little sense into the fool.

"There's two ways this goes, friends," Goss was saying. "You three boys light a shuck for parts unknown, or we do it the hard way. You three get to call the tune."

"*Señor* McKown has done nothing wrong," the Mexican said. "Why should we leave and allow you to do the devil's handiwork?"

The Missourian smiled. "Because you don't want to die."

The black man rose, picked up his canteen and canvas war bag and began walking out of camp, not saying anything, not looking at anyone, just turning onto Front Street across from the empty tents and makeshift cabins and heading south.

"T. J.!" the Mexican called out. "T. J.! Don't run from these fiends."

Beale licked his thick lips, waiting. Next up was the Indian. "Shem!" the Mexican cried.

"Thirty cents a day ain't worth dying for, my friend," the Ute said softly.

Goss waited until the Indian had disappeared behind the trees no one had yet to take an ax to, then checked Front Street. Town was quiet, but it was Sunday morning and most of the citizens were probably still in bed with wicked hangovers from the night before.

The Mexican stood, unwavering, and Beale stepped forward before Goss could turn around and palm his Colt. He didn't know the Mexican, didn't care much for the carpenter one way or the other, but Deke Goss was kill-crazy. He'd pop a cap without thinking twice, and Beale knew that Major Howard didn't want anyone killed today. Just roughed up a little and sent on their way.

"I do not fear you," the Mexican said, and Beale broke his nose with a quick punch. The man fell, cupping the blood pouring from his nose, and Beale lifted the man up with his left hand, and belted him in the stomach with a savage right. He let the carpenter drop to the ground, gasping for breath, choking, snorting blood.

He waited a few seconds, then jerked the Mexican up. This time, to Beale's surprise, the little fellow struck back, placing a well-timed uppercut that split Roland's lower lip. Beale ran his tongue over his lip, tasting warm, salty blood, and smiled.

"This makes it easier," he said, and pitched the carpenter into the two-by-four frames along the courthouse's east wall. Beale moved fast, caught the Mexican before he could fall, and staggered the little man with a series of rights and lefts, hammering the idiot's head, then dropping his punches against unprotected stomach and ribs.

The Mexican slid onto the ground and this time didn't stir. Beale looked around, ignoring the smiling Goss, and grabbed a nearby canteen. He emptied the water on the unconscious man's bloodied face. The Mexican stirred, and rolled into a ball, pleading now in a slurred, broken voice, *"Por favor, señor,* do not hit me again. I will go. I will go now."

"Good," Beale said, and dropped the empty canteen beside the cowering carpenter. The Mexican pulled himself up and staggered away, following his retreating friends.

"Hey, Mex," Goss called out. "If we ever see your face again, or your two pals, we'll kill you. Remember that."

Beale dabbed his bloody lip with his strong fingers and watched Goss gather pine straw and wood chips. "You need me?" he asked the Missourian.

"Nah," Goss replied. "You get outta here and tell the Major what happened. I'll take care of this little tinderbox."

Frank Ivy stepped out of the Montezuma, shielding his eyes from the sunlight. Seventeen hours at the poker table, and two thousand dollars richer. He had won more money in one night, had held better hands, but he couldn't remember a streak this long, this profitable. He wondered how Sam Raintree was faring up at Baldy Town.

He debated trying breakfast at one of the cafes, or getting some sleep. E-Town was quiet on this Sunday morning, and he figured a cup of coffee and maybe some of those hot dishes spiced with a lot of green chiles at the joint called Felipe's would be a well-deserved treat before turning in.

Bootsteps hurried behind him, and Frank had just begun to turn when a giant brushed past him, knocking Ivy slightly against the Montezuma's wall. He started to shout, but checked his tongue. The man kept moving, head down, not looking or caring. Frank doubted if the man knew he had almost trampled someone. Recognition slapped Frank swiftly. The shaved head of the black leviathan, the clenched fists. You never forgot a man that size.

Man-Killer Roland Beale.

The boxer ducked inside the Elkhorn Saloon. What would a fighter like Beale be doing in a place like E-Town? And what would bring him to Major Howard's saloon and gambling parlor? Beale. Remembering the pounding Raintree had taken from those gnarled hands, Ivy felt more relief that Sam had ridden up to Baldy Town.

He brushed off his coat and started down the boardwalk for Felipe's steaming breakfast, pushing thoughts of Roland Beale aside, when he heard the panicked cry:

"FIRE!"

Chapter Nine

It had rained most of Sunday night, turning the already muddy streets into a swamp pit bordered by traps of quicksand. You could lose a Conestoga wagon out there, Frank thought, but a traveler proved him wrong by whipping a heavy freight wagon down Front Street, ripping through the mud like an eagle-claw cultivator. Ivy sat on a bench in front of Joel Lobenstein's Mercantile, scraping off thick clumps of mud off his boots. He almost laughed at his own vanity, the Virginian in him still showing itself after four years on the frontier, primping because his boots had cost him fifteen dollars and not caring that they'd get just as muddy before the day ended unless some entrepreneur starting putting wide planks across the marshy streets.

A woman in blue and white gingham caught his eye

as she carried a crate out of the mercantile and strained to lift it onto the tailgate of a wagon parked in the bog. Black mud swallowed her high-buttoned shoes, and she had managed to angle the crate so that it rested on the edge of the wagon by the time Frank stepped beside her and tipped his hat.

"Allow me, ma'am," he said, and slid the box into the back of the wagon. It was quite heavy. She had to be strong just to have gotten the crate as far as she had. Frank turned around, saw her staring at him with wide eyes. Not in fear, or indignation, but more like she had seen him before. She hadn't. Frank would have remembered her.

Thin yet sinewy, with windswept brown hair and a face bronzed by years in the sun and wind, she wouldn't have been called beautiful, but Frank found her to be pleasant, with an inner strength that came through her fraying clothes and skinned knuckles.

"Thank you," she said, but didn't step away.

"Do you have any more things to be loaded, ma'am?" he asked.

"My father can do it," she said in a fading Southern accent. Her eyes dropped to his feet, then swept past him to the bench and the shavings of mud piled on the warped boardwalk. Ivy realized he still held his cleaning stick, a mud-covered piece of pine, in his left hand.

"Your boots are muddy again, sir," she said, and laughed, leaving him smiling at himself as she went back inside Lobenstein's. He waited almost a minute to see if she returned with another crate, or if her father would need help, but when no one came through the doorway, he tramped back to his bench and scraped off more mud with his stick.

You're acting like you never saw a woman, he told himself, crossing his leg and sending another slab of mud splattering on the boardwalk. Then again, maybe he hadn't really seen a woman, a real woman, in a while. That's one of the hazards of making a career of late nights in smoke-filled parlors and saloons where the only women are hurdy-gurdy girls and painted ladies with opium-laced eyes. Most gamblers slept while the real women and honest workers conducted their business, and Frank would have been in bed right now if he had not been dealing five-card stud from seven o'clock Sunday night until just thirty minutes ago. Sunday evening at a card table. Mama wouldn't have appreciated that.

The woman stepped out behind her father, loading another crate into the wagon, but Ivy's boots occupied his attention now and he didn't notice them until the man stepped onto the boardwalk and bellowed, "Stevens!"

Marshal King Stevens leaned against a railing on the corner of the street, thumbs, as usual, hooked in his gunbelt, and cigarette dangling from his pallid lips. Stick in hand, Ivy glanced at the gunman first, next at the barrel-chested, redheaded man with malevolent eyes. About twenty yards separated the two, and Frank Ivy sat in the middle, the one place no one would want to be right now. He saw the woman, sitting on the wagon seat, mouth open, unmoving. Frank caught another look at her father. He wore no gun.

"What do you want, McKown?" Stevens asked, stepping away from the wooden railing.

A dog barked.

A rooster crowed.

Someone dumped a slop jar or emptied a wash basin from an upstairs room at the nearby Placer Hotel.

And then . . . silence.

McKown. Frank recognized the name. This man, the pretty woman's father, had to be Ian McKown, the carpenter building the courthouse and jail. The structure had burned yesterday morning, reducing two or three weeks' work to cinder, ash and charred pine. That had dominated most of the conversation last night at the Montezuma. *Someone set the fire . . . No, it had been an accident . . . No witnesses. Maybe McKown's hired hands did the dirty deed. After all, they had left town . . . It was a job for the vigilantes . . . No, the vigilantes were probably behind it. McKown will quit now . . . Ten dollars says he doesn't . . . More proof that we need a jail in this town . . . What it's proof of is that E-Town needs a volunteer fire department—this whole valley could have gone up in smoke had the wind been blowin'.*

"You figure on finding the men who put a torch to my jail just standing there?"

Stevens flicked his cigarette onto muddy Front Street. His pale eyes bore into the carpenter, but McKown didn't waffle, his eyes equally intense. Neither man, Ivy soon realized, noticed him. He could have been a June bug for all McKown or Stevens realized. The fact that the carpenter didn't spot him came as no surprise, but a gunman like King Stevens usually took in everyone, everything. Maybe the cat-like killer wasn't so observant, or he was just too cocksure of himself. That lack of caution might get him killed someday.

The marshal took a few steps forward and said, "You claiming it was arson, McKown?"

"You know it was."

"I figured your boys just put too much pitch-pine in their cookfire. That's mighty dangerous, you know. Man's gotta be careful. But if you want me to, I'll see about getting a warrant on them boys of yours. Arson's a serious offense."

"My hired hands didn't do this."

"No? I heard they ran off. That's a sure sign of guilt. I'll get a posse up and we'll mosey down to Cimarron if you want."

"You won't find the men that did this in Cimarron."

"Where then?"

"Try upstairs at the Elkhorn Saloon."

King Stevens lost his smile. His hands moved to the Navy Colts and rested on the ivory grips. "You better watch your step, McKown," he said icily.

"You listen to me you miserable black-heart. I won't be played for a fool by a carpetbagger like Howard or some squat assassin like you."

Stevens roared and charged, pulling one of the Colts and reversing the grip. He didn't plan on killing the carpenter—if that had been the case, he would have just shot the man where he stood—but would beat the man senseless with his pistol. Ian McKown didn't move, just stood waiting for the killer, and Frank told himself that a man that size could take care of himself. Mind your business—a good policy for a gambler— is what Sam Raintree would have said if he were in Ivy's boots, although the Texan probably would have looked to place a few bets on the impending brawl.

Mind your business, Frank told himself once more, but couldn't help but bring his slightly cleaned T. C. McInerney boots into the marshal's path. Stevens tripped, sailing in the air and landing a few steps from

McKown, the .36-caliber Colt sinking into the mud. The killer rolled to his right, reaching for his other revolver, trying to find out who tripped him, but Frank covered the distance in an instant. His right foot shot out, and the boot caught Stevens in the head with a solid thunk. Stevens rolled over, off the boardwalk, and sank face-down into the sludge. He tried to lift himself, let out a slight groan, and dropped again with another splat.

Ivy caught his breath, looked at the stick he held stupidly in his hand and tossed it away.

"I could have handled this, mister," Ian McKown said.

"Yes sir," Ivy said, and tried to think of something else to add but couldn't.

"Anyway, I reckon I'm obliged. But I wouldn't make a habit of sticking your nose into other men's affairs."

"Sounds like good advice," Frank said, wishing he had taken his own before jumping in. "But I guess I had a bone to pick with Marshal Stevens myself."

McKown smiled. At least, Ivy thought he had ever so briefly before the emotionless mask returned. The carpenter held out a hand the size of a ham.

"Ian McKown," he said.

"Frank Ivy."

They shook firmly, and the carpenter nodded to his daughter. "This is Alice, my girl."

The woman was smiling now. Frank tipped his hat again. "Miss McKown," he said, aware that he was staring at her.

He turned, hearing McKown speaking again. "You'd do well to take your leave of E-Town, Mr. Ivy." The carpenter pointed at the unconscious lawman. "Stevens ain't likely to forget the knot you left on the side of his head."

"Thanks," he said, "but I don't think he saw me. I'll be all right."

"Suit yourself, but you'd best be careful."

He watched the wagon churn through the mud down Front Street. When King Stevens moaned again, Frank decided he'd best leave, quickly.

"So you didn't see who turned Marshal Stevens's face purple?"

The quailing little merchant shook his head, and Man-Killer Roland Beale laughed. He didn't know what he found more amusing, the fact that this four-eyed little pusher of overpriced calico and ten-penny nails was about have himself an accident, or the bruised noggin of Marshal King Stevens.

"I just heard a noise, and by the time I got outside, the marshal was just coming to," Lobenstein said.

Beale guffawed again, picturing the proud marshal left wallowing in the mud like a dumb Poland China.

It didn't really matter if the merchant saw what had happened or not. Stevens already knew who tripped and kicked him. But Major Howard did care about something else. He couldn't keep that carpenter from buying wood at the sawmills—Lucien Maxwell had an interest in the mills, and he wielded even more power than the Major around here—or ordering supplies outside of Colfax County, but he could make sure a weakling like this Lobenstein stopped being so friendly with the McKowns. That would make obtaining building material a tad harder.

Beale picked up a nail and fingered it gently. "I think it would be wise if you ended your account with

Ian McKown," he said easily. "Bad for business. Mighty bad." He held the iron nail with thumb and forefinger against the wooden counter, and in a flash brought his right palm flat against the head, driving the nail deep into the counter top as Lobenstein gawked.

The runt would need a claw hammer to pull out the nail, Beale thought as he left the office and joined King Stevens and Deke Goss and walked with them to the alley behind the Montezuma Bar and Club Rooms.

They waited for the sandy-haired gambler to step outside to use the privy, and as soon as he did, Beale wrapped his arms around the man's slender but solid frame. Before the man could start to struggle, Stevens buried his fist in the Southerner's stomach. The gambler gasped, and the marshal pulled out Sandy-Hair's holstered revolver and tossed it aside.

"Assaulting a lawman is a serious offense, Ivy," Stevens said, and slammed a right into Sandy-Hair's temple when he looked up. "Only because of my generosity am I giving you the opportunity to leave E-Town as soon as you can saddle your horse." He lashed out a quick succession of jabs and hooks, and Beale felt the gambler go limp against his body.

Stevens nodded, and Beale let the Southerner fall to the ground. With a smirk, King Stevens kicked the unconscious gambler in the head and turned to leave, barking out a menacing order.

"Finish it."

Chapter Ten

She gasped, unconsciously bringing both hands to her mouth, and stared in horror. The man in the alley behind the Montezuma lay in a supine position in the shadows, not moving, halfway buried in the mud. Her feet made a sucking sound as she moved off firmer ground toward the body, and her heart sank.

"Jeff?" she asked softly, and took a few tentative steps.

Sandy hair, matted with blood and mud, an empty holster and tall boots with fancy inlays. Not Jeff, she realized, and sighed. Guilt quickly replaced relief, and she knelt beside the unmoving figure and stared. The gentleman who had stepped in this morning, had helped her load the nails and then tripped and kicked that lean marshal before he could pistol-whip Papa—not that Papa couldn't have handled it.

"Mister . . ." She had to think of his name. "Mr. Ivy?"

She leaned over him closer and felt his warm breath. That brought forth another sigh. He wasn't dead. Alice rose quickly and hurried to the water barrel at the corner of the building, loosening her bonnet as she ran. After soaking the cloth in the cold water, she went back to the unconscious gentleman, dabbing the congealed blood on his forehead, bloody nose and mustache and lips.

He flinched, stirred slightly, and moaned.

"Don't move," she whispered, and continued to clean his battered face. His eyes fluttered, darted, finally focused on her. When Alice first saw him, he had reminded her of Hugh Morris, handsome, charming, well-mannered. Now he looked nothing at all like the brave Kershaw County planter.

He whispered something, but she couldn't hear. Alice leaned forward.

"Bet wrong," he said weakly, and wet his lips. Alice straightened, stared at him, waited for an explanation.

He swallowed. "Stevens saw me after all," he said, and grinned.

Alice McKown smiled back.

"Are any bones broken?" she asked.

"My head," he answered. "Likely every other bone in my body, too."

His eyes closed. Just the effort of conversation had worn him out, she knew, but suddenly he pulled himself into a seated position before Alice could protest. He groaned, began to weave, and she put an arm around his shoulders to steady him.

The back door to the Montezuma opened, and a portly man with a porkpie hat and sack suit stumbled toward the outhouse, not noticing Alice and the gambler or simply not caring.

"Help me to my feet, Miss McKown," he said through grinding teeth.

"No," she said. "You should lie still."

"I'll be all right," he argued. "If you'll just help me to my room."

He leaned on her, and rather than argue further, she stood with him, slipping once and almost sending both into the mud. His breathing had turned heavy now, and she waited until he nodded his battered head slightly.

"You need a doctor," she said.

"Nearest one's at Fort Union," he said. "I'm at the Moreno. Room Two-oh-four. You don't have to walk me upstairs. I'll make it."

"You couldn't climb two steps, Mr. Ivy, let alone a staircase."

"The clerk will help me."

Alice smiled. What chivalry. He was a gentleman after all, not compromising an unmarried woman by having her seen entering a man's hotel room. They took a step, hesitant at first, then another, stopping to rest at the corner of the Montezuma. She waited for his signal, and their feet tangled and sent them face-first into the mud.

She rolled over and smeared the grime off her face, combed out the clods in her hair with her fingers, then dabbed the gambler's face with the only portion of the hems of her dress that wasn't caked in muck.

"Are you all right?" she asked.

He answered with a brief laugh.

On their feet again, they turned south, climbed onto the boardwalk and dodged past uninterested miners and prostitutes. Ivy straightened before they had gone a block and said, "The hotel's the other way, ma'am."

"I'm not taking you to your hotel, Mr. Ivy," she answered.

"You're a fool," Ian McKown said as the battered gambler sipped the broth Alice had made him. "I figured that Stevens would have knocked some sense into you last night. You should get out of town before he finishes what he started."

The gambler smiled through swollen lips. He had a couple of broken ribs, wrapped with torn strips from some of William's shirts, probably a concussion, yet he was talking about going back to his hotel and staying. What for? A winning streak? He never could understand gamblers, professional or not. Why, Ian McKown had never even bet on a horseshoe-pitching contest.

"Stevens said he'd give me time until I can ride a horse," Frank Ivy said.

"Well," Alice spoke up, "I dare say you won't be doing that for a few days."

McKown shook his head. "I don't like owing debts, Ivy," he said. "But this is your own fault. I didn't ask you to step in and boot that ruffian in the face."

"Yes sir," the gambler said, and lifted himself gingerly off the tailgate and to the ground, steadying himself by leaning against the wagon. The man had guts, McKown said. Most men would have never gotten off the ground after such a beating. McKown smiled.

"I did enjoy it, though," he said.

Ivy's eyes danced with humor. "So did I," he admitted.

"Even now?"

"Even now."

He was all right, this Frank Ivy. McKown handed him a wooden cane he had carved. The gambler took it. "Thanks," he said. "This will help me get back to my hotel."

But Alice had jumped down beside him. "You'll do no such thing, Mr. Ivy. If you insist on going back to your room, I'll give you a lift in the wagon."

"No need for that, ma'am. I've been too much a bother already."

"You haven't been a bother, Mr. Ivy. Now let me help you back up."

McKown turned. He'd let Alice finish up with the gambler. He had best help Conall. As he walked away, he heard Ivy tell Alice, "Thank you much, Miss McKown," and he had to smile when he heard his daughter's reply. "You're quite welcome. And, please, call me Alice."

Three days passed before Frank Ivy felt like venturing out of the Moreno Hotel. He found the Dance .44 still in the alley, surprised no one had stolen it, although caked thick with mud it would have been hard to spot. After stopping for a bite to eat at Felipe's, he returned to Room 204 and spent two hours disassembling the revolver, cleaning and loading it and placing new percussion caps on five of the cylinder's six nipples.

Three days without work, four when you considered King Stevens and his rogues waylaid him fairly early Monday evening. The time had come to end this

forced vacation. He buckled on his gunbelt, an effort
that pained his sore ribs, holstered the Texas-made pistol and pulled on his hat.

The palomino mare remained boarded at the livery.
The smart play would be to pay his bills, saddle up
and ride up to Baldy Town to find Sam Raintree and
either set up a table there or move on. A man like
King Stevens didn't make idle threats, and a seasoned
gambler knew when the time had come to cut his
losses.

He stopped off at the Miner's Inn, which Major
Judd Howard did not own, for a brandy to consider
his options. He still hadn't honestly come to a decision
when he stepped onto the boardwalk in the gloaming
of another June day. He looked across the street and
spotted Alice McKown walking, eyes straight ahead,
not seeing Frank. He liked the way she carried herself.

Ivy smiled, and started to cross the street to say
hello. He stopped, though, when the gambler from the
Elkhorn rushed up behind her and took her arm. Alice
spun, startled, and grinned at him, playfully slapping
his arms for the scare. Both laughed, and ducked inside an alley.

The brandy flittered in his stomach. Jealousy. Frank
couldn't remember the last time he had felt that emo-
tion, perhaps not since Betsy Mae Stewart said she
couldn't dance with him at the Lexington Summer So-
cial because she had promised all waltzes to Cadet
Eugene Price.

That should have been the determining sign, the
hole card that would send Frank Ivy to the livery and
up Baldy Mountain. What had Alice's father called
him? A fool? Yep, the carpenter was right. Frank Ivy,
Licensed Fool. A man can't live forever, he told him-

self as he walked down the street, away from Damaso's Livery and toward the Montezuma Bar and Club Rooms where he was renting a table for fifteen dollars a night or five percent of his winnings, whichever was greater.

"I've missed you terribly," Jeff Rowley told her. "I came by Monday, behind the Montezuma, but you weren't there."

"Something came up," she said. He didn't need to know about Frank Ivy.

He grinned wickedly. "It's been too long. We have a lot of catching up to do." He started to pull her close, but she pushed away.

"Jeff," she said, hating the weakness sounding in her voice. "I need your help."

"That's what I'm here for, Alice. Anything you want."

She felt better hearing that. "It's Papa," she said, and Jeff nodded, understanding. "Mr. Lobenstein won't sell us any more supplies. I don't know why— he's always been good to us."

"That is strange," he said. "Would you like me to talk to him?"

"I don't think it would do any good. Papa thinks he's scared of Major Howard. I was hoping—and I'm not asking for money or anything—but, well, Papa is too proud to ask for help. But he and Conall can't build the courthouse by themselves."

"What about your other brother?"

She choked out a humorless laugh. "James? Not hardly."

"Would you help us?" There. She had said it. And

it made her sick—mainly because she knew how Jeffrey Rowley would answer.

"I'm no carpenter," he said, releasing his grip on her shoulders and putting his hands in his coat pockets, not even looking at her anymore. "And your father wouldn't have me. I'm sorry, Alice. Really. But you don't need me. You father wouldn't want me there. And besides, what is there to do? If Mr. Lobenstein won't sell you goods, how can you finish the jail?"

"Papa has more supplies coming. They should be here in a day or two."

"More supplies?" He was suddenly interested, looking up from his feet. She stared deeper into his eyes. He seemed different now, not a paramour but something darker. "Where are they coming from, Alice? Cimarron? Colorado?"

What did it matter? Dark suspicion clouded her face, but Jeff Rowley didn't seem to notice. Alice thought back. When the building had been burned— Jeff knew they would be gone that morning. No one else did, except the hired carpenters. Jeff did deal for Major Judd Howard. And what did she really know about him, other than he made her feel good with his promises and kisses? She thought about herself. Here she was, meeting a man in alleys in the early evening, far from proper. Why? Because she was ashamed of him, or was he ashamed of her? Was there a clandestine side to her new beau? Now she felt foolish.

"Papa ordered them from Santa Fe," she said. "I imagine that means they'll arrive from the Cimarron Toll Road."

"In a day or two you said."

She nodded, knowing now. "Two days. But you know how freighters are."

Chapter Eleven

Ian and Conall McKown took the last load of one-by-six planks off the back of the freight wagon and laid the freshly cut timbers on the stack beside the building. Hard work for two men, Alice thought, and the least the two men who brought the load from the sawmill could have done was help Papa and Conall stack it. But, no, they just sat on the wagon and watched, which was why Alice forgot about her Camden upbringing and did not bother to offer either of them a drinking gourd. They still sat there on the seat of the wagon like two pieces of dead juniper, while Papa ducked inside his Sibley tent to pay the men. Conall splashed water on his face, then took a long drink, before climbing up the steps and heading inside the building.

A minute later, she heard his hammering. He could work forever. In fact, Alice often had to make him knock off for dinner or supper.

With just the two of them—three if you counted the times they would let Alice drive nails or work a hand-saw—they had made a lot of progress reframing the foundation and putting up the two-by-four studs and braces after clearing the ruins and debris from the fire. The novelty of the construction site had lost its appeal, and few visitors or spectators showed up these days. That suited all of the McKowns just fine.

Papa was taking too long. The men from the saw-mill were beginning to get restless. About the time Alice decided to check on her father, Old Iron-Headed Ian pushed through the dirty canvas and walked to the wagon, holding a pouch in one hand and a small scale in the other. He weighed the gold on the back of the wagon, then filled a leather pouch with the appropriate amount and handed it to the thin, balding driver.

As the wagon pulled away, Papa carried the scale and sank into a wooden camp chair near Alice. She handed him a cup of coffee without his asking.

"Thanks, little girl," he said wearily, resting the scale at his feet.

"You all right, Papa?" she asked. Once he could outwork Conall, or anyone else for that matter. He needed to realize that he wasn't a young man anymore.

"Tired," he answered, honest for once. "Plumb tuck-ered out." He sipped the coffee, nodded in satisfaction, and jerked his head slightly toward his tent.

"Think you could take my scale back to the tent?" he asked.

"Sure," Alice replied and picked it up.

"We could use some more gold," he said. "Our finances are dwindling, and we'll have a substantial bill when the supplies get here tomorrow or the next day."

"I'll go talk to James this evening." That was Papa, too proud to ask James for money.

"You're a good girl, Alice. I'm mighty proud of you."

"And you're working too hard, Papa. You and Conall both."

"Yeah," he said. "But it'll be worth it in the end."

Man-Killer Roland Beale took his customary spot on the far wall of the Major's office and listened to that uppity gambler explain what he had found out from the carpenter's daughter. What a cretin, this Jeff Rowley, pretending to woo some innocent gal just to feed Judd Howard's greed and ego. Beale didn't see what it mattered if some dreamer built a courthouse or not. So the Major lost his hold in the Moreno Valley? He couldn't keep killing and cheating honest folks forever. Pretty soon, they'd get sick of him and run him out on a rail. And then he'd be free to find some other mining camp to milk and bleed.

What a miserable lot I've joined, he thought. But the Major paid well, and Beale had nowhere to go, not home, unless he wanted to head back east to visit the parents he had shamed, if they were even still alive, or turn himself in to the New York City constables and be fitted for a hangman's noose. He glanced at the other vermin in the office: the dwarf from Missouri, Deke Goss; that half-breed named Gideon who never said a word; and Marshal King Stevens, with his bruised forehead and black eye. That made Beale smile.

"Beale! What's so funny?"

He frowned and straightened, looking at the Major and mumbling some sort of an apology. "I'm listening, Major," he said.

"You'd better be. Now, do you know if that gambler's still in town, the one who made our good marshal take a bath in the streets?"

"He got lucky!" Stevens shot out. "That's all."

Beale checked his grin. "Yes sir," he answered. "He hasn't left yet. Saw him just last night at the Montezuma, dealing stud."

Stevens shuffled his feet. "He'll leave soon, one way or the other. I can still charge him for assault."

"And then have him shot trying to escape?" Major Howard took a long swig from his tumbler, shaking his head. "Don't press your luck, Stevens. If you wanted to arrest him, or kill him, you should have done it that very day. He's no threat to us. But McKown is."

The major took another drink, wiping his mouth with the back of his one hand. "Supplies are coming up from Santa Fe?" he asked Rowley.

"That's what she said."

"The Cimarron Toll Road then," he said. "Goss, I want you and the breed to take care of that. You'd best hurry. If he ordered the supplies from Santa Fe, they'll be coming in on Judah Miller's freight wagons." He smiled. "I hear tell there have been a lot of bandits robbing travelers in the Palisades."

Deke Goss grinned. "I hear that, too."

"Make sure of it," he said.

They were dismissed. Beale went down the stairs and out the door. Personal. Major Howard didn't fear the courthouse and jail; he simply hated that carpenter McKown. John Adams Wilson, alias Man-Killer Roland Beale, didn't understand hate. He stopped, staring at the tall man in buckskins riding down Front Street. Beale never forgot a face, especially the face of a man who had once shamed him, cost him his career with Martin Simon.

Dallas, Texas, January of '68. Beale snapped his fingers as the name came to him. Sam Raintree. He had hammered that Texan as hard as he could, but the old Reb never fell, although he spat out a lot of blood and teeth and both of his eyes were swollen shut by the time the bell rang to end the final round.

Beale's black eyes followed the tall Texan until horse and rider disappeared inside the livery. Roland Beale had thought about quitting the Major, just leaving the fifty dollars a month and letting his long legs carry him back to Fort Union, maybe Santa Fe or down south to La Mesilla. But Raintree's arrival changed all that. No, Man-Killer Roland Beale didn't understand hate, but he certainly understood revenge.

"Let me see that."

Reluctantly, James McKown held out his bandaged left hand, and watched as his sister unwrapped the torn strip of underwear and shook her head. She stood, never releasing her grip on his wrist, and guided him into the lean-to he had built after Papa, Conall and Alice left the claim, taking with them the tent he and Conall had shared.

"I know you've got some whiskey in here," Alice said. "Let's have it."

With a sigh, he nodded toward a box holding his skillet, coffee pot and plates. Alice reached behind the crate and withdrew a half-full bottle of the cheapest liquor he could find for sale at the Crazy Ute. He sat on his straw bed, and flinched as Alice wasted more whiskey than she needed on his hand.

"What were you waiting for, James?" she asked, and began tearing strips off her petticoat. "Gangrene to set in so they could chop off your whole arm?"

"It's nothing," he answered, shaking his hand now that Alice had freed it. "Just cut myself fixing a sluice box."

"Uh-huh."

She wrapped her bandage around his hand, too tight, he thought. She looked around his home, showing her disapproval. What did she think he could build out here, alone? A duplicate of their two-story home back in Camden?

"Yeah, I know," he said. "It ain't much to look at, and Conall and Papa would laugh at it. But it beats sleeping on the ground like I was doing the last time you visited."

Alice's dark eyes looked up. He saw her smile. "That's not much of a roof, James," she said. "And you're still sleeping on the ground."

He stood, taking the remains of his whiskey and corking the bottle. "Let me guess, sis. You're here for gold."

He lifted his bedroll, found two pouches and tossed them to her. Alice caught them. She stared, saying nothing.

"Well, go on. Take 'em back to Old Iron-Headed Ian." She hefted the pouches, and he swore. "I know. It's not as much. Well, tell Papa and Big Brother that I'm not cheating them. Either the claim's playing out, or I'm as bad a miner as I am a carpenter."

"James," she said, her voice softer, her green eyes tearing. He had hurt her feelings. Well, she had hurt his. James McKown was keeping this family fed by sweating eighteen hours a day over this claim, panning and digging for color, scraping by while Old Iron-Headed Ian, Conall and Alice worked on some stupid building, a fool's dream. He could make more money shoveling out the livery stable than working here, but no one, even his family, cared. They just came to visit once in a while to take their share of the gold, working until it hurt to bend his fingers, until his back refused to bend, even cutting his palm with a hatchet to repair a sluice box.

"Get out of here," he snapped. "Go back to where you belong."

Chapter Twelve

His feet hurt, so Isidrio Adán Pascual Silvestre left the road, climbed down the boulders and fallen trees and sat on the banks of the Cimarron River, kicking off his dust-covered, battered sandals and submerging his dust-covered, blistered feet into the shallow but fast-flowing and chilling water.

"*Bueno*," he said, leaning back and listening to the conversations of squirrels or chipmunks. Tall trees rustled in the wind, and Isidrio wondered how far he had walked this day and how long it would take him to reach this famous *ciudad* they called E-Town. Until this morning, he had never ventured past the stone quarry near his father's father's adobe home except to go hunting or fishing or to take a load of bricks to the village of Cimarron. But now, with the blessing of his mother if not his father and brothers, he was on his own, *a mano*, free to find his fortunes in this E-Town. He would become rich, yes, and come back to build his mother, and brothers and father also, a home that would put the home of *Señor* and *Señora* Maxwell to shame.

He pulled a sopapilla from the canvas sack slung over his shoulder, and ate it hungrily. It needed honey, but honey he did not have, so he sat up, cupped his hands and drank the cold water. His father would expect him home soon, not believing that this sixteen-year-old lad could find his way to the Moreno Valley even though this road led straight to the garden of gold. Nor did his brothers or the villagers of Cimarron believe in young Isidrio Silvestre.

Pobre muchacho, an old man had told his domino partner at the table outside the store, *me pregunto qué será de él*. The words ran through Isidrio's head once more. Poor boy, I wonder what will become of him. He laughed, and said to himself, *Old man, I shall become rich. That is what will become of me.*

His stomach grumbled. The sopapillas his mother made were already gone, and still he was hungry. E-Town lay far ahead, so he slipped on his sandals and climbed back to the road, picking up the dead limb of a tree to serve as a cane in case his feet began to hurt more.

He had gone another mile, maybe two (he hoped three or four), when his swollen feet forced him to rest on a boulder. The sun warmed his face, and he closed his eyes, praying to the Virgin Mother that this place called E-Town would be just around the bend. An eagle screeched and left its nest somewhere in the rugged, windswept cliffs that shot above the green forests into the clear blue sky.

He was thirsty, but the river seemed too far. He didn't know if he could climb down the banks and back up again. *Zonzo*. He should have brought a canteen with him. The squeaks and groans of a wagon reached his ears, and he straightened and looked down the road. Six jennies pulled a wagon covered with canvas, while a man in a funny hat sat with the reins in his arm and whistled. He watched the donkeys and driver, none in any hurry, approach. Another *norteamericano, muy loco*. Did not he understand that strong horses, mules or oxen should pull wagons, not burros?

"Whoa," the man said, tugging on the reins until the wagon stopped beside Isidrio. The *norteamericano* pushed back his tall black hat, the kind he had seen in the photograph of the dead president called Lincoln. "Afternoon, my friend," the wagon driver said. "You look all tuckered out."

Tuckered out? He did not understand this. "*Buenas tardes, señor.*"

The driver smiled. He dressed like a rich man, with a linen duster to protect his fine suit from the dust of the trail. "Do you speak English, my friend?"

"*Sí.*" Isidrio felt like a fool. "I mean, yes, *señor*. I speak English . . . *un poco.*"

"Well, great. Where are you walking to, my friend?"

"E-Town. I mean, Elizabethtown."

"Excellent. That's where I'm bound. I would be happy to give you a ride. The name is Jonathan R. Ferguson. I'm starting a newspaper in Elizabethtown. *The Moreno Lantern*, I've decided to call it. Hop aboard, my friend."

Isidrio hesitated. "I could not impose, *señor.*"

"It's no imposition, friend. I haven't enjoyed the company of anyone since I left Albuquerque, and I certainly could pick the brain of a native such as yourself to get a feeling for this beautiful country."

Pick the brain? He would never understand these *norteamericanos*. But his feet felt raw, and even a burro-pulled wagon seemed better than walking. "*Muchas gracias, señor. Mucho gusto.*"

"You're welcome. And the pleasure is mine."

So, this newspaper editor understood Spanish, at least a little. "I am Isidrio Adán Pascual Silvestre, *señor*. You may call me Isidrio."

"And, as I said, I am Jonathan R. Ferguson, and, please, call me Jon." Isidrio tossed aside his walking stick, walked around the wagon and climbed onto the seat next to the editor.

Ferguson flicked the reins, and the donkeys began pulling the wagon.

They didn't make good time, not because of the burros, but because this editor would stop and stare in wonder at anything—the sunflowers beginning to bloom on the roadside, a mule deer grazing nearby, a hawk gliding through the air—scratching strange marks on the books of blank paper at his feet, and saying *loco* things to no one.

A white cloud floated over the pointed peaks as they dipped into the canyon, and once again, the editor stopped the wagon and pointed to the cloud. He said:

> *I wandered lonely as a cloud*
> *That floats on high o'er vales and hills,*
> *When all at once I saw a crowd,*
> *A host, of golden daffodils.*

Wrapping the reins around the brake he had just set, he leaned down and retrieved his pencil and writing paper. "That's William Wordsworth," he told Isidrio. "Have you heard of him?"

"No, *señor*."

"Does this place have a name?"

Isidrio looked up, confused. "*Sí*," he said at last comprehending as *Señor* Ferguson looked at the towering canyon walls. "It is called the Palisades."

"Palisades," the *norteamericano* said and wrote it down on his paper. "Monzonite, I'm betting. Volcanic rock." He winked at Isidrio. "I learned this, Isidrio. Journalists learn things; we aren't professors. I met a geologist at Fort Union. Interesting fellow. Monzonite, but I have to admit, I like Palisades better. From the French, if I'm not mistaken. It looks like an irregular picket fence painted light brown. A stockade of volcanic rock made by God. Do you see the wonder, the beauty of this country, Isidrio?"

"*Sí*," he answered, not knowing what else to say.

And the *norteamericano* said: " 'One touch of nature makes the whole world kin.' That's Shakespeare, *mi amigo, Troilus and Cressida*." He returned his paper and pencil to the floorboard, grabbed the reins, released the brakes and whipped the donkeys into movement once more.

The motion of the wagon, combined with the warming sun and Isidrio's fatigue, rocked him to sleep. He was dreaming a good dream—ordering servants to serve his mother *lechón asado, papas y zanahorias*, instead of her burning her fingers feeding her husband, sons and the rich *gringos*—when the wagon lurched to a stop, jerking him awake. The brake screeched, and *Señor* Ferguson swore and leaped off the wagon seat.

Isidrio rubbed his eyes and gasped when he saw the wagon on the side of the road, four oxen dead in the yokes, one man face-down in the dirt and another leaning against the rear wheel of the freight wagon. Canvas tarps covering the merchandise had been ripped apart, boxes broken open and items flung about like hungry dogs would going through a trash pile. Slowly, mechanically, Isidrio climbed off the wagon, kneeling to make the sign of the cross above the dead man, a boy of his own heritage and perhaps his own age.

Who would do such a thing? he wondered. Perhaps the Jicarilla Apaches or Moache Utes. He saw the cans with drawings of peaches on the white labels littering the road, and wondered why the Indians had not made off with the food. The unopened cans reminded him of his hunger, and he rose. Picks, shovels, plates and more tins of food had been strewn about. He picked up another tin, but this one had no drawings, just the letters he had never learned. Placing it on the wagon near another broken crate, he quietly approached *Señor* Ferguson, who had knelt by the black-bearded *norteamericano* and was tying a white shirt around the man's bloody belly. The bearded man with glassy eyes let out a moan as the newspaperman tightened the knot.

"Did you see who did this?" *Señor* Ferguson asked.

"Yeah," the man said. "They thought I was dead. Killed ol' Donnie, then . . ." He cried out before continuing. "Shot our oxen from the trees. Hit me. Then came out." He groaned.

"Indians?" the editor asked.

The bearded man shook his head. "White. Well, one

of 'em could have been Mex or Injun. Couldn't see good. Madder than a hornet, one of 'em was. Little guy. Started goin' through packs and crates, cussin', sayin' . . ."

Señor Ferguson turned to Isidrio, saying, "*Amigo*, bring a canteen. *Muy pronto, por favor.*"

Yes, he would be happy to get away from this bleeding man, but the bearded *hombre* shook his head and said, "Don't bother wastin' water on a dead man."

Isidrio stopped, turned back to the ugly scene and crossed himself twice.

"What's your name?" the editor asked.

"Tom Blair. My pard's name was Donato Franco, called him Donnie."

"Anybody you want me to write?"

He shook his head. "Donnie and me didn't have no family, just freightin' for Mr. Judah Miller down in Santa Fe."

"Anything else you can tell me about the men who did this to you?"

"Kept yellin' 'Where is it?' Cussin' up a storm. Figured they waylaid the wrong wagon." He tried to laugh. "That's my luck."

The newspaperman stood. "Mr. Blair," he said. "I have a little Kentucky sour mash in my wagon. It might ease the pain."

El hombre nodded, and *Señor* Ferguson told Isidrio to wait with the freighter while he ran awkwardly, holding his tall black hat with one hand, and disappeared behind the wagon. Isidrio sank beside the bearded man.

"What's your name, boy?" he asked.

"Isidrio Adán Pascual Silvestre."

"That's a mouthful. Glad you and your *amigo* happened along, *muchacho*. Didn't fancy dyin' alone." He pulled a bloody right hand from his stomach and offered it to Isidrio, who took it hesitantly. He was still holding the freighter's hand when the newspaperman returned.

"Mr. Blair?" *Señor* Ferguson asked.

Isidrio released the man's hand and rose. "He is dead, *señor*," he said, crossing himself again and saying a silent prayer.

The newspaper editor took a sip from the tall bottle, while Isidrio ran through the trees to wash his hands and cry. As the Cimarron River carried the blood and Isidrio's tears downstream, he vomited. Fifteen minutes or so later, he stumbled back to the road where *Señor* Ferguson leaned against the front wheel of the freight wagon, bottle by his side, and scribbled furiously on his papers. He looked up when he heard Isidrio and said, "Murder in the Palisades."

Isidrio stared harder. These *norteamericanos* were strange men, said strange things. "*¿Que?*"

With a smile, the man took another pull on the sour mash and said: "My first headline."

Chapter Thirteen

Judd Howard sent a backhand across Jeff Rowley's face, the slap sounding like a pistol shot in the Elkhorn office. "That's what Alice told me—" the stupid Ohioan began, and Howard slapped him again. He felt the blood rushing to his head and wanted another drink. What he really wanted, though, was smart men, and here he stood surrounded by his best thugs, the only one of them worth a spit being Marshal King Stevens.

"I don't care what she told you!" Howard boomed. "You got lied to. I thought you gamblers could read people's faces." He shook his head in disgust and stared at the small Missourian, Deke Goss.

"And you," he continued. "Two men killed for nothing." He pulled the folded newspaper from his coat pocket. "Did you see this?" Of course not. Deke Goss probably couldn't read. "You gave our new newspaper editor a walloper of a story. 'Murder in the Palisades.' " He flung the four-page premiere edition into the gunman's face. What he really wanted to do was slap the dwarf, but Goss, unlike that craven coward Rowley, might not take that from any man. "What were you and that half-breed thinking?"

"We were told it was one of Judah Miller's wagons, and that's what we hit. Recognized the driver."

"But he wasn't carrying McKown's supplies, was he? You shot first, then looked through the wagons. Fools!"

· A week had passed since the editor discovered the dead freighters, and he had been asking Howard, as mayor, and Stevens, as marshal, what they planned on doing about it. Oh, King Stevens had ridden out with the vigilante committee twice only to come back empty-handed. And now this journalist, Mr. Jonathan R. Ferguson, had filled the front page of his *Lantern* with something other than an editorial on what he planned to give readers, subscription information, a plea for news, tidbits from around the Territory and a few stupid quotations from Shakespeare, Milton and the late Abe Lincoln.

Murder in the Palisades!
Two Freighters Killed by Bandits
Your Editor, Mexican Youth First
On the Scene
Shocking Brutality
One Man's Dying Words
Marshal Has No Suspects
What Can Be Done To Stop This Outlawry?

What left bile in Howard's mouth wasn't just the stupidity of those two numskulls Goss and Gideon. But the very next day, two wagonloads of supplies had arrived at McKown's construction site. That petticoat had suckered Rowley good. The wagons came from Trinidad, Colorado, coming down Raton Pass at Willow Springs and taking the toll road to E-Town. Never trust a woman, Howard had always said.

Old McKown had plenty of wood, shingles, and all sorts of tools to finish his stupid jail and courthouse. Although he still didn't have the furniture—benches, chairs, and the like—bars for the jails, and stoves. Those would have to come from Missouri, more than likely, and wouldn't be here for a month or two. It would be hard to have a jail without any bars, Howard thought, and he probably could make sure the Reb's next batch of supplies didn't make it to E-Town.

"What do you want us to do, Major?" Goss asked.

Howard sank into his chair with a sigh. The Missourian looked ready, eager to please, while Jeff Rowley tested his reddened cheek. King Stevens fired up a cigarette.

"There's nothing we can do now," Howard said.

"We can fix another accident," Goss suggested. "Send McKown's place up in smoke again. Bet he'd quit then."

Howard shook his head. "Leave McKown alone for a while. He's not going to get much done with just him and his son working. We need this Palisades thing to be forgotten, so I don't want to give the *Lantern* editor anything to write about, something that might stir up our good residents." He reached for his decanter, filled his tumbler and looked at Rowley. "Although, Jeff, you might think about teaching your lady friend some manners."

"Eight bets," Frank Ivy said and looked at the eight of hearts face-up across the table.

Sam Raintree took a peek at his hole card and bet ten dollars. They were playing five-card stud, had been going at it for almost forty hours now, and what once had been a game involving seven players had dwindled to two, Sam Raintree and Frank. Others had bowed out because of a lack of funds or they were just too tired to continue. Seventeen hours ago, the Montezuma had been full of spectators watching the game. Now, only the newspaper editor, bartender and a couple of others watched. Frank looked at the seven of clubs showing, then bent the corner of his down card. Seven of diamonds. He bet ten, and raised twenty. Sam Raintree called.

Ivy dealt Raintree a five of diamonds and turned over the king of spades for himself.

"Fifty dollars," he said.

"You won't run me off with that obvious bluff." The Texan tossed in five blue chips. "Call."

Three of diamonds for Raintree. Six of hearts for Ivy. One card left, and providing Raintree had not paired up already, he needed another eight to beat Frank.

"Keep it at fifty, Sam."

He pushed a stack of chips into the center of the table. Raintree sent a stream of tobacco juice into the nearby spittoon and bet fifty, and raised fifty. The newspaper editor sucked in air through his teeth. Ivy studied his friend. Was he bluffing? Or had he paired up the eights with the first two cards and had been sandbagging?

"I call," Ivy said, and added fifty dollars in chips to the pot.

He slipped off the queen of clubs to Raintree and dealt himself the two of diamonds. No help. And now Sam's queen concerned him.

"Fifty dollars," he said.

"I call," the Texan said and turned over the ace of diamonds.

Frank let out a sigh. "Pair of sevens," he said, and raked in his winnings. He tried to guess his total. It had to be close to two thousand dollars, and Sam had won probably fifteen hundred. E-Town had been good to both of them.

Alice had traded her worn copy of *The Old Curiosity Shop* for half a dozen eggs, cured bacon and a loaf of bread. Papa had spent his savings on this courthouse and jail, and any gold James worked out of the claim also found its way to other men's coffers for shingles, nails, saws and wood. She probably could have gotten a better deal for a Charles Dickens book— even with the new paper, reading material was scarce in the valley—but she didn't want to spend too much time in town. She hurried down the boardwalk, weaving in and out of the throngs of people, using her apron as a basket to hold her plunder.

Someone jerked her from behind, sending the bread, bacon and eggs flying into the alley, and before she could scream, a hand clamped over her mouth. Someone laughed as she struggled, but it wasn't her kidnapper, just a drunken miner who probably thought she was a prostitute being pursued by an overeager customer. The man behind her released his grip and hurled her forward against a rain and garbage barrel. She had been here many times, behind the Montezuma, and even before she turned around and heard the angry curses, she knew her attacker.

"You lied to me!" Jeff Rowley snapped.

Alice waited, hoping some good Samaritan would follow her into the alley, but no one did, the E-Town legions either in too big a hurry to spend their wages and pokes or too afraid to get involved. She was on her own.

"What of it!" she fired back. "You've been lying to me for I don't know how long."

A feeling of nausea began to match her rage. She had suspected Rowley of being one of Major Howard's spies, and now she knew for certain. This also meant that those two men hauling supplies from Santa Fe had been murdered because of her. Jeff Rowley—how could she have been infatuated with him?—was responsible, too. She wondered if he had actually killed the two freighters in the Palisades.

"Is this what I get?" Rowley shook with anger. "Is this what you want? We could have gone to San Francisco together once I had a stake."

She laughed bitterly. "I wouldn't go as far as the Cimarron Toll Road with you, Jeff," she said, and swore. The curse surprised Rowley. He probably had never heard such language from a "proper woman," and maybe it surprised her, too, but she was a long way from Kershaw County.

"Then go back to that dirt-poor daddy of yours," he said. "Go back driving nails and slopping hogs. You had a chance to be something with me, Alice."

"A concubine?"

He stepped closer, and she saw the malignant darkness in his eyes. Yet she refused to back down. "I bet the law would be interested in my story, Jeff. You asking about our supplies, and then . . ."

This time, Jeffrey Rowley laughed. "Go tell Marshal Stevens."

That stopped her, but only briefly. "I bet that newspaper editor would believe me."

He lunged, catching her off-guard. His small hands tightened against her throat, thumbs pushing down hard, forcing her against the wall. She couldn't breathe. Rage masked his face, and she couldn't break his hold or scream for help. She lowered her hands. Rowley didn't care, too focused on choking her. She found the butt of the derringer in his vest, jerked it out, cocked the hammer and pushed the barrel into his stomach.

That caught his attention. He took a few steps back, releasing his grip, and Alice fought for air, careful not to lower the hideaway gun. When she could speak again, she told him: "If you ever touch me again, I'll kill you."

He seemed to be breathing just as hard as she was, so she hurried down the alley, dropping the derringer as she ran. Mistake. He tackled her. She rolled over, and he slapped her, sweeping the derringer into his right hand. Alice closed her eyes.

Frank Ivy's boot caught the gambler in the temple and sent him sprawling, the derringer sailing a few yards from the miserable snake. The man shook his head and sat up slowly, while Frank helped the McKown girl to her feet. She brushed herself off, and said nothing.

"Excuse me, ma'am," Ivy said, and walked to the gambler—one of Major Howard's dealers—and kicked him in the stomach. He would have kicked the rogue all the way to Texas if Alice hadn't said something. When Frank turned toward the woman, he heard the gambler moving. Ivy whipped around, drawing and cocking the Dance. The gambler had dived for the derringer, but stopped where he lay, little gun in his tiny hand. His face, now drained of color except for the quickly forming bruises and blood dripping from his busted lip, turned.

"You've got one shot with that pop gun," Ivy said, "and I have five in this .44. You're a gambler. What are your odds?"

The man's hand left the derringer in the dirt, and he slowly stood and wobbled down the alley, away from Front Street, disappearing in the shadows. Frank holstered the revolver and approached the carpenter's daughter.

"You all right, ma'am?"

"Yes," she said. She thanked him and walked toward Front Street, too proud or scared to stay here longer. Ivy had stepped outside to nature's call after a long poker game, and was supposed to meet up with Raintree at Felipe's, but Sam Raintree could wait. He caught up with the girl at the end of the alley, saw her brushing off a dirty loaf of bread and a slab of bacon. He knelt beside her and picked up two eggs. Four more were busted.

She looked at him, her face expressionless although her throat was reddened. Ivy checked his rage. He wanted to go after that two-bit gambler and throttle him. Any man that would mishandle a woman. . . .

"Thank you, Mr. Ivy," she said, and rose, lifting her

dirty apron. Frank, understanding, placed the two eggs on the piece of cloth.

"I'd like to walk you home, Miss McKown," he said.

"That's not necessary," she answered. "I'm all right. And Rowley won't bother me anymore."

"I know," he said. "But I'd like to walk you home anyway."

Chapter Fourteen

"Y ou've made a lot of progress," Ivy told Mr. McKown, as Alice brought him a cup of coffee. He sipped the drink and refrained from making a face. He wondered how the McKowns were making their coffee these days. Burning grain and boiling water? It had been years since Ivy had tasted coffee this bad, not since the War when he'd ride into Yankee lines under a flag of truce to swap Virginia plug tobacco for Federal coffee.

Ian McKown nodded with tired pleasure. "It's mighty hard going sometimes, but Conall and I—" he smiled at Alice—"and my daughter, too. We're getting it done. Conall and Alice will be mighty proud of it all when it's finished."

"You, too, Papa," she told him.

He ignored her praise. "It's not every day that we get visitors, Mr. Ivy."

"Call me Frank."

"Frank it is, then. I'll be mighty happy to give you a tour, but it's getting late and I wouldn't want you stepping on a rusty nail."

"Some other time, then," Ivy said. "I'd like to see it."

He sipped more coffee, pleased with himself. He had finagled another invitation to the McKown camp, and this worked out well. He could leave now and meet Raintree at the cafe before the Texan flew into a rage.

They chatted for a few more minutes, and Frank took his leave, shaking McKown's massive hand, waving at McKown's son, still hammering away on the slanted roof, and tipping his hat at Alice before walking down the road.

You are acting like a lovesick schoolboy, he told himself. A former Virginia horse soldier *walking* instead of riding, just to be near a young woman who probably doesn't care if you exist. He saw a Mexican youth in front of the Moreno Hotel, holding up newspapers and yelling out something in broken English. Frank had heard about *The Moreno Lantern*, had met the editor in the Montezuma—a pretty good gent for a Yank—but he had yet to read a copy of the newspaper.

He stopped in front of the teen-ager and asked for a copy.

Pleased, the young boy handed Frank the first edition. Frank scanned the front page headlines: "Murder in the Palisades!" . . . "News From Around The Territory" . . . "Subscription Information" . . . "A Plea For

News" . . . and, at the bottom left corner of the broadsheet, "Editorial Statement of *The Moreno Lantern*." Frank read that first:

Our founding fathers knew the power, but also the responsibility, of the press, and as the editor of *The Moreno Lantern*, I vow to you to cover the news of Elizabethtown and the Moreno Valley with fairness to all. I am a Republican, having served under General Grant during the late war, but I likewise respect the beliefs of Democrats and former Confederate soldiers as much as I respect the beliefs of Catholics, Protestants, Jews, Apaches, Utes, atheists, as well as drunks and temperance crusaders. Many journalists slant their newspapers to their own doctrines. I will not.

A multifarious culture has descended upon this golden Garden of Eden. Hear your neighbors. If we listen to each other, if we work together, if we respect each other, we can make Elizabethtown a great place, a city that rivals Athens, Rome, Chicago and Charleston.

I stand for law and order, for justice, for the freedoms our forefathers granted all of us. I am happy to serve you, and I shall always remain
Your obt servant,
Jonathan R. Ferguson,
Editor & Publisher
The Moreno Lantern

Frank looked up, realized he had not paid the Mexican boy for the newspaper. He fingered a nickel in his vest pocket, and then pulled out a twenty-dollar gold piece.

"I cannot change that, *señor*," the newspaper hawker said.

"That's all right. I was wondering if you could do me a favor."

The boy's eyes fell to the glistening coin. "*Sí, señor.*"

"I'd like for you to go to the grocery across the street, and buy some coffee, sugar, beans . . ." He paused, thinking. He had seen a clay pipe on the wagon seat back at the McKown camp. "Pipe tobacco," he added, and tried to think what Alice would want. A dress or something of that nature would be too forward, too presumptuous. "A dozen eggs," he said, "and maybe some canned peaches or pears. Can you handle that for me?"

"*Sí.*"

"Spend fifteen dollars. Then take them to the camp at the end of town, where two men and a woman are putting up a building. Do you know where I mean?"

"*Sí.*"

"That'll leave you five dollars. That's for your trouble." The boy's eyes widened. "Take the supplies to the girl. Do not give them to the men." Ian McKown wouldn't accept the gifts. Too proud. Ivy was certain of that, but Alice might. "Tell them it is in appreciation of Miss McKown's service to Mr. Frank Ivy." She would have to know where the food came from before she'd take it. Those McKowns were as stubborn as Frank's own family.

He looked at the Mexican. "You do speak English, don't you?"

"*Sí.* I mean, yes."

Frank began to have his doubts, but the boy threw his shoulders back and looked determined. "I am Isidrio Adán Pascual Silvestre, at your service, *señor*. I will take coffee, beans, sugar, peaches, pipe tobacco and pears to the people. This I promise you."

Ivy smiled. "And a dozen eggs, Isidrio."

The boy's eyes fell to his well-worn sandals. "Oh, *por favor*. Forgive me, *señor*."

"It's all right," Frank said, and pressed the coin into the boy's dirty hands. "You'll do fine."

Isidrio Adán Pascual Silvestre did not like the look in the eyes of this *señorita*. He hoped the *norteamericano* with the fine suit and gray hat had not been playing some type of joke. He hoped the woman would believe him, and that he would not ruin the man's message. *La señorita* peered in the heavy crate he had struggled to keep from dropping on the long walk from the grocery to this strange camp. Beyond the woman, two men worked on a long saw.

"Who sent this?" the lady asked.

Isidrio took a deep breath. "It is in a-a-a . . ." He knew he was in trouble. He had disappointed the *norteamericano* with the sandy hair already. He would never earn the trust of that rich *hombre*, and would be stuck in this crowded city earning a few pennies by selling newspapers once a week. Isidrio had not found much luck in this E-Town. No one would hire him at the mines for he had no experience in mining, and other places told him they had no jobs. If it had not been for the newspaperman, Isidrio knew he would now be back with his father, mother and brothers, hearing their laughter at his stupid failure. The newspaperman, though, gave him a place to sleep and a few pennies for selling the papers, but Isidrio found out that he did not have the makings of a newspaperman. He could not read what the papers said, and the money he made did not buy much food for his stomach. Of course, he would never tell the newspaperman that for food, he dug through the trash cans behind the log buildings. Just being in the grocery today and buying all the food for this woman made his stomach groan. Perhaps tomorrow he would treat himself to a breakfast of *huevos rancheros* with the five dollars he had earned from the *norteamericano*—providing the man did not demand the return of his money.

"Well?" the *señorita* said.

Isidrio tried again. "It is in appre—" What was that word? "Appre . . . Ah-pre-she—"

"Appreciation?"

Bueno. The *señorita* came to his aid. "*Sí.* It is in appreciation of Miss Mac—"

"McKown."

"*Muchas gracias, señorita.* I am but a poor, dumb boy. Forgive me for my . . ."

"It's all right."

"But I no remember more of what the man said. I am sorry."

Yet this lady smiled at him, even offered him a slice of the bread he had bought. He took it gingerly. She still smiled. "I think I know," she said.

Isidrio turned, hearing the voice of a towering man with red hair, followed by another giant, although a younger man.

"What's going on?" the older man asked.

"Nothing," the lady said.

"I'll be jiggered," the younger giant said. "Where did that grub come from?"

"This boy brought it," the lady said.

"Why?" the older man said.

Isidrio did not know how to answer. He thought this big man might throw him all the way back to Cimarron. "*Señor*," he found himself saying. "I am the son of a stonemason. I am very strong for my size, but there is little work for me to do in town. I have been selling newspapers today for the editor-man, but I . . . well, today . . . I . . ."

"Son," the giant said. "Do you want a job?"

Isidrio paused, and blinked. This had not been his plan. He had merely meant to explain his hardships, and tell why he had shamed himself and the carpenter and his family by bringing the food from the *norteamericano*. And now . . .

"You didn't have to bring us what's left of your food, son." This came from the young man. "But if you want to throw in with us, being a stonemason isn't much different than being a carpenter. We'll pay you back for the grub."

The older man nodded his massive head. "That's right. We pay thirty cents a day and food. You can start first thing tomorrow."

Isidrio Adán Pascual Silvestre almost wept.

"I think," Sam Raintree was saying, "that we've just about milked this town like a turnip. Three cards."

Ivy dealt three red-and-white-backed cards. They sat alone at a table in Felipe's, dealing five-card draw to each other to pass the time while waiting on green chile stew. Frank looked at his own hand. King of diamonds, jack of clubs, three of spades, four of clubs, five of spades. Good thing they weren't playing for money. He kept the face cards and dealt himself three more.

"What you got?" Raintree asked.

Frank glanced at his hand. "Pair of jacks."

"Beats queen high. Anyway, I was thinkin' about headin' to Abilene. Be a bunch of Texas waddies and Chicago beef buyers in town, and we could clean up."

It made sense, and followed Ivy's own rules. Never stay in one place too long, no matter how much you had won. Yet Frank wanted to see Alice McKown again. He found himself thinking a lot of his own father and brother, his forgotten years as a carpenter, and there was something noble about a man like Ian McKown, building a courthouse and jail for the people of the valley, to honor his dead son. A man doing something with his life, not wandering from town to town living off the turn of a card.

He passed the deck to Sam, who dealt. "How many?" Raintree asked.

Ivy picked up his cards and smiled. "I'm pat."

Raintree shook his head in disgust. "I'll take three." The Texan dealt his draw and smiled. "Two pair," he said, laying down the cards. "Queens and jacks."

Frank nodded. "Straight," he said, and showed his hand: five of diamonds, six of hearts, seven of diamonds, eight of hearts, nine of hearts. "We are playing straights and flushes, right?"

"Yeah. Only we ain't playin' for money. Good thing, too. You ain't lost in a coon's age. Let's go to Kansas, pard, and I'll take you down a peg."

"I'll give you a chance to take me down here, Sam." Raintree grinned. Frank wasn't even sure why these words came out of his mouth. "No poker. No luck. Just me and you."

"You ain't talkin' 'bout fightin'. You ain't that loco."

"No. But you remember that carpenter building a courthouse and jail?" Raintree nodded. "I bet I can outlast you working for him. We work until the building's finished. If I quit first, you win. If you can cut it, then I win."

"How much?"

"Let's make it interesting," Ivy said. "Five thousand dollars."

"It's a bet."

Chapter Fifteen

He had his doubts about the two men, even Frank Ivy, and Ian McKown liked the gentleman gambler. Still when Ivy brought the buckskin-clad Texan to camp and said they both wanted to go to work, McKown arched his eyebrows and crossed his arms. Conall had the Mexican boy sawing planks, and Isidrio showed he was no stranger to hard work. But gamblers? Ivy and Raintree certainly didn't have calloused hands dealing cards. And they had a lukewarm reason for seeing this job complete.

A bet. Well, at least they had been honest. Ivy and Raintree were betting on who could last the longest. Neither of them could outwork Conall or himself. In fact, he didn't think they would last as long as Isidrio. He figured Ivy took the bet to be closer to Alice, and, to his surprise, that really didn't bother him. But the other motives troubled him, because while this might be a game, a friendly wager, to the gamblers, the Elizabethtown Courthouse and Jail meant much more to Ian McKown.

"Either one of you have any carpentry experience?" he finally asked.

"Yes sir," Ivy replied. "Before the war, I worked for my father building houses in Virginia. I admit it's been a while, sir."

McKown turned to the Texan. Sam Raintree spit out tobacco juice, wiped his mouth and answered, "I've put up a few lean-tos, dug my share of post holes."

He frowned. This wasn't a barn or corral. He saw the makeshift work table near the wagon, a few one-by-eight planks resting on two saw horses. Pointing to the New Langdon Box he had ordered from Trinidad, he asked, "Do you know what that is?"

Raintree scratched his cheek. "Some kind of fancy saw box," he said.

Well, that was one way of putting it. McKown's gaze moved to Ivy, who seemed to be stifling a laugh. "It's a mitre box," Ivy said. "Used for joints. You can cut at angles from right angles to forty-five degrees."

McKown nodded, impressed. He thought about quizzing the two on block planes, augers, ratchet braces, plumbs, levels, chalkline rules, keyhole calipers and combination squares. He could go on all day with that, but figured it would be a waste of time. Still, he wasn't quite convinced. He told the two men to follow him and walked to the bench, pressing a finger at the bottom floor of the courthouse design.

"What's that?" he asked.

"It's a blueprint," Sam Raintree answered proudly.

This time, McKown had to suppress a laugh. "I mean, what I'm pointing at."

Ivy leaned forward. "Door opening," he said. "You'll have a sole plate on the bottom, plus top plate with king and jack studs at the door's sides, and a double header and cripple stud above the door. Pretty fancy for a frontier town."

The Texan spit again. "I suppose you learnt all that at VMI?"

"Not hardly," Ivy replied.

Now, McKown's interest had been piqued. "You attended the Virginia Military Institute?"

"Yes sir. Class of '60."

"And you fought in the war?"

"Sixth Virginia Cavalry."

McKown nodded with approval and looked at the Texan. Without having to be asked, Raintree said, "Hood's Texas Brigade. And I got through the fifth *McGuffey's Reader.*"

Ian McKown laughed for the first time in ages. "All right, so this is just a bet between you two?"

Both answered, and McKown, still smiling, said, "Well, to be honest, it's a bit of a gamble for me, too. Ivy, you've shown me you know about carpentry. We'll see how you hold a hammer. Mr. Raintree, what can you show me?"

The Texan spun, saw Isidrio struggling to carry another plank to his work station and walked quickly to the stack of wood. He squatted, picked up a load of the eight-foot planks and followed the Mexican. The youth was half-dragging, half-carrying one plank. The Texan hefted at least half a dozen, maybe more.

"He'll do," McKown heard himself saying. "You'll both do."

*   *   *

Sam Raintree swore, slammed the adze-eye hammer on the floor and stuck his swelling thumb into his mouth.

With a laugh, Frank drove another nail into the plank and said, "I've told you before, Sam. You're not holding your mouth right."

He couldn't recall the last time he heard that joke. Eight years? *Hold your mouth right and you'll hit the nail, and not your thumbnail.* That had been the first bit of advice his father ever gave him about carpentry work. It seemed hard to believe, but Frank was enjoying himself. He liked the way the hammer felt in his right hand—better than the .44 Dance, even better than a broken-in deck of Steamboat Playing Cards. The aroma of sawdust pleased him. And he wore the symbol of a carpenter, a pencil stuck above his right ear.

"You want to quit, Sam, go right ahead," Ivy joked.

Raintree removed his thumb from his mouth. "You ain't runnin' me off, Ivy, no matter how many times I break this thumb."

At first, when Frank and Sam knocked off work, they went back to the Moreno Hotel. Sometimes they'd share a drink or find a card game, but the McKown workload started making that form of entertainment an unwise proposition. By the end of the first week, Frank had checked out of the hotel and was sleeping underneath the wagon next to Isidrio. Raintree refused to give up his comforts, so Ivy spent an hour or so each night practicing his poker skills by teaching Isidrio the game.

"That's not much of a hand," he told the Mexican after dealing the queen of diamonds, ten of diamonds, nine of hearts, six of hearts and five of diamonds.

"*Sí,*" Isidrio replied. "The lady is a good card though, no?"

"It's a queen." He watched as the Mexican counted the number of diamonds and hearts. You didn't have to read English to play poker.

"I should keep the lady and the ten, no?" he asked.

"That's what I would do. And if the betting got out of hand, I'd fold." Frank laid down his own hand. "I have a pair of jacks. I'll discard these." He put the queen of hearts, eight of hearts and seven of diamonds on the center of the table.

"You would throw away the lady?"

"On this hand, yes. Queen isn't doing me any good. I'd have a better chance of drawing three cards and maybe matching my jacks. You understand?"

"*Sí.*"

Frank dealt three more cards up for Isidrio. Four of diamonds, king of diamonds, nine of diamonds. He stared at the boy's hand in disbelief, and swore.

"*Señor* Frank," Isidrio said. "What does this mean? All of my cards have diamonds on them. Is it a mistake?"

"I wish it was, Isidrio," he said, and dealt himself the ten of hearts, two of hearts and jack of clubs. "Because you would have taken me for quite a lot of money with that hand. It's called a flush, and providing you are playing straights and flushes, you win."

"*Bueno.* How much do I win?"

Frank laughed.

"Isidrio," Alice McKown said from the campfire, "don't think about becoming a gambler. My mother always said that cards are the devil's tools."

Ivy recalled his mother saying the same thing.

* * *

The newspaper editor showed up on Saturday, July 3, bringing his latest edition of *The Moreno Lantern*. "Thought you might enjoy this," *Señor* Ferguson said, tipping his tall hat at the *señorita* and handing the newspaper to *Señor* McKown. "How do you like your new job, Isidrio?"

"*Muy bueno.*" Isidrio was glad this newspaperman did not dislike him for taking another job. When Isidrio said he planned to work for *Señor* McKown, the editor said he understood and added that Isidrio would always be able to sell the *Lantern* if he so desired.

"Good, good," *Señor* Ferguson was saying. "I found a little waif to hawk my papers, but he's not as dependable as you, Isidrio. When this jail is complete, maybe you'll come back to work for me. I could use a printer's apprentice."

Isidrio did not answer. He did not know what one did as this "printer's apprentice," but it seemed certain that one would have to understand the language of the *norteamericanos*. The editor did not wait for an answer, much to Isidrio's relief, and turned to *Señor* McKown, saying: "I'd like to know what you think of my editorial on page two."

Isidrio's boss handed the newspaper to his daughter, saying he didn't have his reading spectacles with him, and asked her to read the editorial out loud. That made Isidrio glad. He wanted to know what made *Señor* Ferguson happy and did not want to reveal his ignorance and shame by having to ask someone to read this "editorial."

Señorita Alice cleared her throat and began:

In the last week as I put this edition of The Moreno Lantern *to bed, there have been two mur-*

ders, including one lynching, fifteen assaults and seven robberies reported to this office. Doubtless, this number will increase before you read these humble words.

Yet for all of these crimes, Marshal—and I use his title dubiously—K. Stevens has arrested no one, and our mayor, Maj. Howard, has done nothing within his powers to bring about some semblance of justice.

For the six thousand of us calling the Moreno Valley home, we should feel outrage at our officials. I am told that Marshal Stevens and Deputy Goss are investigating these crimes, and the Vigilante Committee will make these fiends pay for their outlawry. But I wonder: What clues can be our good Marshal and able Deputy find in the whiskey demijohns sold at the Crazy Ute?

Perhaps many of us do not care. I do not believe that those among our population still living in canvas tents and dugouts plan to remain in our fair city through the winter. But some of us want to call E-Town our permanent home. We want to build for the future, for our families. But what can we have when ruffians are free to do as they please, our mayor is more interested in his profits from his gambling establishments and houses of ill repute, and our duly appointed marshals and deputies would rather drink and play keno than enforce the laws of New Mexico Territory? And where is this so-called Vigilante Committee that I have heard so much about but have yet to see?

Perhaps you have noticed the courthouse and jail being constructed by a fine Southern gentleman and his family at the edge of town. Mr.

McKown is building this at his own expense, as a memorial to his youngest son, hanged by those Vigilantes who are allegedly enforcing the laws but might well be breaking them.

Mr. McKown is to be commended for his sacrifice, for his desire. Even a suspicious fire that destroyed most of the building has not deterred him. He tore down the debris and started over. But the construction of a courthouse and jail is just the start. A frame building does not automatically give a community justice.

I am reminded of the words of Christ as told by Luke. "He is like a man which built a house, and digged deep, and laid the foundation on a rock: and when the flood arose, the stream beat vehemently upon that house, and could not shake it: for it was founded upon a rock. But he that heareth, and doeth not, is like a man that without a foundation built an house upon the earth; against which the stream did beat vehemently, and immediately it fell; and the ruin of that house was great."

The Elizabethtown Courthouse and Jail can be the foundation of the law in the Moreno Valley. But without a true desire for justice, without the backing and support of our good men and women, if we continue to let murderers and thieves roam free, the ruin of Elizabethtown will be great.

Señorita Alice folded the paper, and her father said, "Mr. Ferguson. You're a Yank, but I must admit that I like the way you write."

Chapter Sixteen

"Yankee holidays ain't somethin' I care to celebrate," Raintree had said, and Frank couldn't convince the Texan that he would be celebrating Mr. McKown's birthday, not the Fourth of July. But Sam could be mighty stubborn. "It's McKown's misfortune to be born on such an unfortunate date. You have fun. I'll find a card game somewheres."

So Frank Ivy found himself in company with Isidrio and the McKowns, except James, still looking for gold and ignoring the Sabbath. They walked toward Baldy Town before stopping in a meadow more than a mile from E-Town. Frank's feet hurt. His Abilene boots weren't meant for traipsing all over New Mexico Territory, so he was glad to sit on the grass and watch

as Alice spread fried chicken, some cheese and biscuits on a wool blanket.

"No birthday cake?" he quipped.

"Afraid not. Papa never has had much of a sweet
tooth."

More than likely, they couldn't afford the eggs, but-
ter and sugar that went into such a luxury. Ivy picked
a blade of grass to chew on and looked toward Baldy
Mountain. It was Sunday, and Independence Day, but
he still heard the pounding of sledgehammers from
miners and the wail of the sawmills. In the distance,
a yoke of oxen pulled more tall pines from the hill-
sides toward the sawmill. He wondered how long it
would be until they stripped this valley of trees. When
he looked back, he saw Ian and Conall McKown, followed by Isidrio, walking toward a stream, carrying
cane fishing poles and a can of worms.

"Where are they going?" he asked, although that
was obvious.

"Fishing, silly," she said.

"Aren't they hungry?"

"The food will keep. Papa said he wanted to have
fish for supper. It is his birthday."

He sat up, saw Alice handing him a drumstick, and
took it, realizing they were alone. Ivy wondered if Ian
McKown really wanted trout for supper, or if he just
felt like giving his daughter privacy. He bit into the
drumstick, trying to recall the last time he had tasted
fried chicken, wondering how much a chicken had
cost the McKowns in E-Town, and thinking that, if he
were Alice's father, he would have left her giant of a
brother here armed with a shotgun.

Frank tossed the finished drumstick into the grass

and washed the meat down with a canteen filled with tea. His eyes fell upon Alice, kneeling opposite him, smoothing her fraying gingham dress with her hands.

"You remind me of a man I . . . knew," she said.

"I'm flattered."

"He died at Gettysburg."

Ivy took a slow breath, exhaled. "I'm sorry. My brother died there, also."

A long silence filled a space of perhaps a minute, neither one knowing what to say. Finally, she spoke. "Why are you and Mr. Raintree helping us?"

"It's a bet," he said with a smile. "Five thousand dollars." He regretted mentioning the amount. Alice McKown probably hadn't ever seen five hundred dollars. Any money she and her family might have earned went straight to the courthouse and jail. He didn't want her to think he was flaunting his temporary wealth. Ivy knew he could lose his New Mexico winnings quickly once his luck turned. But she didn't seem bothered by the money.

"That's not the real reason."

Frank pushed his hat brim up. "I am a gambler, Alice."

She continued to stare, not satisfied with his answer. Perceptive. Proud, not fishing for a compliment.

"I wanted to be near you," he said, surprised by his honesty. She would go now, get up without comment and follow her father to the stream. But she didn't. Instead, she looked away from him, no longer fiddling with her dress, and shook her head.

"Frank . . ." It came out as a whisper. When she looked up, she said, "I'm a poor choice . . ."

He crawled across the blanket, expecting her to bolt, but she simply watched him. He wanted to take her in his arms and kiss her, but knew she probably had loved that gambler from the Elkhorn, or thought she had, and he could sense her sadness at the loss of whomever it was that fell at Gettysburg.

Give it time, he thought. Don't rush things.

"Alice," he said, "you are a wonderful woman, a strong woman. And it's the Fourth of July, your father's birthday, a beautiful Sunday, and this is a picnic. Do you know what we should do?"

"What?" Her lips quivered.

He stood, pulling her to her feet as he rose, and smiled, jerking his head toward the stream. "Celebrate. I'm wearing boots, but I think I can outrun you to that stream."

"Are you making a bet, Mr. Ivy?" she asked, smiling now.

"Absolutely. I'm a gambler, remember?"

"All right. And the loser has to push Conall into the water. On three." She turned, shouted "THREE!" and took off, lifting her dress as she ran, giggling like a girl. Frank called her a cheater and took off after her, knowing he wouldn't catch her, even if he had tried.

Man-Killer Roland Beale waited for the big Texas gambler to step out of the Moreno Hotel. The big ox picked his teeth with a toothpick and looked up, spotting Beale, and slid the tiny toothpick into the dingy hatband on his ugly hat.

"Remember me?" Beale asked, cracking his knuckles with a smile.

" 'Course," came the reply, "I remember most of the ugly faces I've whupped. Especially . . ." Beale let the Texan go on, full of braggadocio and invectives, showing his ignorance and fear. For once, Beale would enjoy earning his pay from Major Howard.

When the Texan finally paused for breath, Beale said, "I'd like a rematch."

"Good," said the Texan. "You got a time and place in mind?"

"Right now. Right here."

The Texan unbuckled his gunbelt, removed his jacket and hat, laying them on the hitching post in front of the hotel, and stepped off the boardwalk.

"Is this another one of them two-round jobs, or is it till only one's left standing?"

Beale ran his massive right hand over his freshly shaved head. "I won't need two rounds," he said, and dodged the Texan's first punch.

Raintree's fists hadn't softened, and he punched just as hard as he had back in Dallas a year and a half ago. Beale gave the tall Reb credit for that. He felt sweat mingling with blood as he danced around Front Street, aware of the crowd now circling both men, chanting, swearing, placing bets, drinking, cringing at the sound of blows, the crunching of cartilage.

This wasn't anything like the boxing Mr. Martin Simon had taught Beale. He likened it to two old long-horn bulls going at it, trying to prove who would be king of the herd.

Beale sent another roundhouse right to the Texan's head, but Raintree blocked it. A left to the jaw. That staggered Raintree, and Beale moved in. Fake a right. Jab a left. Fake. Right. Right. Right. Left uppercut. All at the Texan's head. Raintree was retreating now. The crowd had to part to give the fighters room. Someone patted Beale's back as he went through the throng, reminding Beale that he still wore his Sunday-go-to-meeting coat and best shirt, now drenched with sweat and splattered with blood.

The Texan delivered a vicious haymaker that staggered Beale, but as Raintree caught his breath, Man-Killer shot out with his left, breaking his opponent's nose. Beale swung around and crashed with his right. Raintree fell, rolled over and pulled himself quickly to his knees by the horse trough. He took time to dip both hands in the water and wash his bloody, dirty face.

Heaving, but in need of a break himself, Beale removed his coat and shirt, tossing them to a smiling Gideon, who stood in the crowd. Someone handed Beale a mug of beer, which he drank in two swallows, and he dropped the empty glass and took a few steps toward Raintree. Putting both hands on his knees, he waited until his breathing steadied, and called out, "Had enough, Reb?"

Raintree rose, weaving, and took a swig from a bottle someone gave him.

"Not hardly," he said, and came after him.

The Texan swung, a glancing blow off Beale's left shoulder. Beginning to tire, Beale thought, and resumed his attack on Raintree's head. Left. Left. Right. Fake. Left. Jab. Right. Uppercut. Jab. Jab. Jab. Fake. Right.

"Stop this!" someone shouted. "Stop this brutality on the Sabbath."

"Shut up, Corbett," came the reply. "We's just celebratin' the Fourth of July."

"Yes, certainly," an Irish brogue followed. "This is a gentlemanly display of prizefighting, under the old Broughton's Rules of 1743."

Right, Beale thought, as he blocked a weak left.

Gentlemanly. No one in E-Town knew the meaning of the word, and he certainly wouldn't call this prize-fighting, no matter what those Broughton's Rules—whatever they were—said.

He knew he had this fight won, providing he didn't make a stupid mistake. The Texan's left eye had already swollen shut, and his punches, while they still might render another man unconscious, were lessening. Beale sent a series of lefts and rights against Raintree's face, letting the big gambler block them with his clenched fists and thick forearms.

Enough. Now! Beale brought a roundhouse right, lowering his delivery at the last second, and crushed the Texan's unprotected ribs. That staggered Raintree, and before he could recover, Man-Killer buried two quick lefts into the stomach. Raintree tried to double over, but Beale caught his torn shirt front and straightened him.

"Finish him!" someone shouted.

Man-Killer Roland Beale didn't need the encouragement. He slammed his right into the Texan's jaw, then forced him against the wooden column in front of the Elkhorn. Right. Right. Right. Beale held the bloodied gambler up with his left hand and pounded him with his right. He doubted if Raintree remained conscious, but on and on he struck.

He heard the murmurs, a few curses and a rising of boos from the spectators.

"That's enough. You kill him, they'll string you up." Beale stopped, recognizing the voice of Marshal Stevens. He released his grip on the Texan and watched him slide down the post and topple over onto his side.

Someone cut loose with a Yankee hurrah, and another man shouted, "Drinks are on the house, boys, at the Crazy Ute!"

Beale wiped his face, spit out saliva, blood and what might have been a tooth, leaned onto his knees once more, and fought for breath. Men slapped his sweaty back, offering congratulations, while others cursed him and sulked away. When he finally straightened, little Deke Goss gripped Beale's right wrist and raised his arm.

"The champion!" Goss declared, and more cheers exploded from the people who hadn't retired to the saloons.

Beale turned around. King Stevens was kneeling over Sam Raintree's body. The Texan opened his one good eye, blinked. "Mister," the marshal said in a hoarse whisper, "can you hear me?"

"Yeah." Raintree's answer was weak.

"Your horse is saddled and waiting for you at the livery. We've already paid your bill at the hotel, and packed up your possibles. Money, too. We ain't thieves. Now, you'd best get out of town."

Deke Goss complained. "I ain't sure he can fork a saddle, King."

"He can ride," Stevens said. "He'd better ride, if he has to lash his wrists to the saddle horn. 'Cause if you can't ride, Tex, I'll let Man-Killer finish this fight."

It surprised Beale, how Raintree pulled himself to his feet and weaved and wobbled down the street. He washed his face in another trough, put on his hat, and moved on, dragging gunbelt and buckskin jacket in the dirt, slowly making his way toward the livery.

"Reckon he'll really leave?" Goss asked.

"Wouldn't you?" Stevens replied.

Chapter Seventeen

Frank
You win. See you at a table sometime.
Your friend,
Sam R.

Ivy read the note in Raintree's almost unreadable scrawl over and over, trying to make some sense out of it. He found a few brown stains at the corner of the note, perhaps dried blood. Alice had found the envelope, addressed to Frank, on the wagon seat Monday morning and handed it to him as he sipped his morning coffee. Raintree hadn't shown up for breakfast, so Ivy had already begun to think something had happened to his friend. But he hadn't expected this, a terse note stuck in with several Yankee greenbacks, yellowbacks, a few gold coins and a five-hundred-dollar check payable to bearer. Ivy didn't have to count the money. He knew all five thousand dollars would be there.

Something had happened. The dried blood told him that, but the note was genuine. No one could forge Sam's handwriting, and few people knew about the five-thousand-dollar bet. Sam had gone. Perhaps he had been beaten, but he had fled Elizabethtown. Frank didn't have to check the Moreno Hotel's register or Damaso's Livery. Captain Sam Raintree, who had led his men against almost certainly impregnable Union forces at Gaines's Mill, Second Bull Run and Antietam, who had never backed down from a fight or wager, had run.

He crumpled the note and tossed it into the fire.

Alice watched Frank walk away from the camp, kicking a triangular wood scrap angrily, and march down Front Street, away from town. She knew what the note said without having to read it. The big Texan was gone. Frank Ivy had won the bet—five thousand dollars—which should make a gambler happy. Her father would miss Raintree's strong back, but she hoped Frank wouldn't go now. After all, he hadn't started working here because of a bet. That had been an excuse.

"Daughter?"

She looked up at Papa, smoking his clay pipe filled with tobacco Frank Ivy had purchased.

"I've never been one to butt my head in my children's businesses," he said, "but if I were you, I'd walk with him."

Alice caught up with Frank and slowed beside him,

trying to match his long strides. At this rate, he would be in Cimarron by nightfall and never once look up. She called out his name, and he noticed her, still walking, before at last he stopped and sighed heavily.

"I'm sorry," she said.

"It's not your fault."

"I know."

The wind picked up, and she let the breeze fill the silence. He unclenched his fists and rested both hands on his hips.

"What bothers you?" she asked tentatively.

She had to wait a couple of minutes before he answered. He looked down the road, then back toward town and finally at her, formulating his answer, trying to understand his own emotions. Maybe he wouldn't tell her. Maybe he thought it was none of her business.

"That he was my friend," he said. "That he couldn't look me in the eye, had to leave a stupid note."

"Maybe he had no choice."

He shook his head. "That wasn't it. Besides, this wasn't about a bet. You know that. He knew that."

She took his right hand in her own. "We don't need him, Frank. We can finish the courthouse ourselves."

"I know."

"Don't be hard on Sam, Frank." The wind picked up. "Do you plan on leaving now? You've won your bet." She braced herself for his answer.

"I'd like to stay," he said. "See the job done."

She smiled, pleased. "I'd like for you to stay, too." Her stomach fluttered. After Hugh Morris, and especially after Jeff Rowley, she thought she wouldn't feel this way about any man. But here she stood, hoping he would bend and kiss her. He did, too, briefly, still the gentleman, still maybe doubting his own feelings for her. Good. Taking it slow. Not rushing anything.

He straightened, still holding her hand.

"We'd better get back," she told him. "Papa pays for a full day's work, and he won't appreciate your gold-bricking."

Sandy-Hair and the Mexican kid slid down the makeshift ladder—or whatever carpenters called it—on the steep-pitched roof and drove two five-penny nails into more wood shingles. The place looked like a real building now, Roland Beale thought, with the walls up, and at the pace Sandy-Hair and the boy were setting, that roof would be finished soon.

The gambler put another shingle in position, plucked a nail from his mouth and swung the hammer hard. Deke Goss found it pretty funny, that all of the carpenters wore aprons around their waists. "Come back next week," the ignorant Missourian said, "and they'll be wearin' dresses." But Beale knew the aprons held nails and other tools maybe, pretty convenient. He found himself almost admiring Sandy-Hair. The gambler had ignored Marshal Stevens' threat and now drove himself with a purpose, driving nail after nail into shingles under a blazing August sun. He wondered if those ribs he had cracked back in June still hurt the gambler.

"You reckon that gent on the roof would listen to reason?" Moss asked, nodding his ugly head toward Sandy-Hair.

"Don't think so," Beale replied.

Earlier that morning, the Major had pulled tightly on his paper collar as if he were choking. He had sworn up and down the office, slamming the rolled-up copy of the latest *Moreno Lantern* against his thighs. That editor was stoking the fire, making things a little hot in the valley for the likes of the vigilantes, King Stevens and the good mayor himself. A month had passed since Beale had sent that Texas blowhard packing—and that had tempered the Major for a spell—but now he was in his cups before noon, foaming and spitting at Ian McKown and that blasted courthouse.

Beale had expected to be ordered to teach the newspaper editor a lesson, but for some reason the Major focused his rage on the carpenter. Maybe it had something to do with the fact that Jonathan Ferguson was a Yank, and Ian McKown an old Rebel. Maybe it had everything to do with that. So once again, Major Howard wanted that building stopped.

"Don't see how," Deke Goss said. "If you don't want us to burn it down."

"No. We can't burn it. Not twice. That'd would give Ferguson too much to write about. He'd demand my head, say I'm worthless as a mayor." Major Howard tossed the *Lantern* into a garbage can. "But you can't have a jail without jail cells. Those haven't been delivered yet."

Goss shrugged. "Reckon so."

"So make sure they aren't delivered. Stop them— and don't botch the job like you did the first one."

So Goss and Beale stood opposite the construction site, watching the carpenters and that woman scurry about. The noise of the hammering and sawing gave Beale a headache.

"How 'bout the Mex boy?" Goss asked.

Beale shook his shaved head. He had done some pretty rotten things in his life, but he hadn't sunk to the depths of Deke Goss. Roughing up some poor teen who couldn't afford boots—well, Roland figured he had a spell to go before he took that trail. "I got a better idea," he told the little killer. "Follow me."

James McKown poured another ounce of color into the leather pouch before tightening the drawstring. He should have done that last night, but instead he had gone to the Crazy Ute for a bottle. Alice had made her usual visit, took the bulk of James's hard-earned gold, and left after another fight. So James felt like getting drunk, and he had.

He heard the snorting of a horse, tossed the pouch on his bedroll and picked up the .31-caliber Manhattan he had picked up in town after Old Iron-Headed Ian, Conall and Alice took off to town. Thumbing back the hammer, James stepped out of the lean-to and turned to face the visitors.

"Howdy," a runt of a man said.

They were an odd couple, this rail-thin dwarf riding a blue roan, and a massive black man on foot. The white man gestured at James's revolver.

"Ain't very friendly," he said.

"What do you want?" James asked. He kept the small revolver cocked, although the barrel remained pointed at the ground.

"Just to talk," the man said, and swung down from his horse. He dropped the reins and took a few steps in front of the animal. The black man followed.

"Before you get smart," the little fellow said, "you might want to take a look over yonder."

He pointed south, and James turned, saw another man leaning against a tree, rifle or musket aimed right at him. Robbery, James thought, and swore underneath his breath. He let the Manhattan fall onto the pine straw at his feet.

"That's more friendly."

James looked up. "You won't get much here," he said.

Both men laughed. "We ain't interested in your poke, friend," the white man said. "Don't want you to think we are law-breakers. Far from it. Truth is, we come to give you a job."

"Job?"

"That's right. Your daddy—he interests me and Man-Killer here, and our boss. We just need some information from you."

James shook his head. "You're asking the wrong person. They don't tell me nothing, and I don't ask."

"Well, you could." The black man had said this, the first words he had spoken. James looked up into the man's scarred face. "Man-Killer," the runt had called him. The name certainly fit.

"I don't understand," James said timidly, suddenly tasting last night's whiskey in his mouth.

"Oh, you savvy," the little man said. "You just need to get friendly with your family again, friend. Work with 'em some. And when you find out stuff that might interest us—like when the next wagonload of supplies is comin' in—you tell us. Easy way to earn money—lot more than you're gettin' out of this stinkin' claim."

The black man, Man-Killer, walked forward, not stopping until he stood toe-to-toe with James. James felt the sweat now.

"If I don't?" he asked weakly.

Man-Killer grinned. "There's two ways we can do this," he said. "Either one's fine and dandy with me.

How do you want to do it?" For emphasis, the giant cracked his knuckles.

James's throat went dry. He could use some more of that wretched whiskey. "How—how do I find you?"

"We'll find you," the white man answered.

James nodded. Man-Killer slipped his right hand into his coat pocket and brought out a leather bag. His huge paw dwarfed the pouch, and he tossed it a few inches. It jingled as it disappeared in the hand. The black man smiled and dropped the pouch at James's feet.

"Payment in advance," he said. "Your thirty pieces of silver."

Chapter Eighteen

Judd Howard felt so pleased he figured it was cause for a drink, so he splashed three fingers of forty-rod into his glass and took a healthy swallow. Deke Goss and Roland Beale had earned their keep this month. Howard had to give them credit. He never would have thought of going to McKown's ostracized son and persuaded him—through fear and bribery—to provide some information every now and then.

Right now, two wagonloads of freight bound for Ian McKown sat waiting outside of Winston McClure's freight yard in Cimarron. King Stevens and Deke Goss had made a rather convincing argument to the freighters, and McClure, that the wagons should stay put. If McKown wanted them badly enough, he'd come get them, and Stevens and Goss left Beale in Cimarron to make sure that didn't happen.

No violence. No scathing article in the *Lantern*. Nothing.

Besides, he had a good reason for stopping the wagons. Ian McKown owed three thousand dollars on that merchandise. It made sense for a businessman like McClure to make sure he saw payment before sending the wagons on to Elizabethtown. That's what King Stevens told the freight man. And Howard knew McKown certainly didn't have three thousand dollars. His son's poor claim wasn't producing that much, and McKown had already spent all of his cash on his stupid building.

Howard thought about taking those wagons and selling off the merchandise, but he couldn't see much of a profit in crates of strap hinges, locks, latches, doorknobs, screws and bolts, plus doors, blinds, transoms, trimmings, window glass, benches, lanterns, iron-barred windows and doors, and, if Goss knew what he was talking about, two Acme heaters and assorted pipes. Maybe, once he had run McKown and his white-trash family out of the valley, he would bring in the wagons and hire someone to finish *his* courthouse. Those heaters would come in handy in a couple of months.

That might make up for letting that big Texan leave with all of his money after Man-Killer had whipped him. Howard hadn't cared too much for that idea, especially with the size of the gambler's winnings, but King Stevens had said it was better this way, less fodder for that newspaper editor, less reason for that big Texan to come back.

Deke Goss tapped on the door—Howard easily recognized the knock—so he sat down and told the deputy to come on in. Howard kept smiling until he saw the Lilliputian holding his ugly hat in both hands. That was always a bad sign.

"What is it?" Howard barked.

"Well, sir, that McKown boy. He was in his daddy's camp last night and said McKown was sendin' someone to Cimarron to see what the holdup was on them wagons."

Holdup. Howard snorted at the word choice.

"We knew that would happen sometime," he said. "Who's he sending? Did the boy know?"

Goss nodded. "Yes sir. Said it'd be that gambler, the one Stevens didn't run out of town. Think the Mex kid's goin' with him."

Howard shot down the rest of the whiskey, still happy. "Good," he said. "We'll kill two birds with one stone. I don't think Beale will have any problems. Do you?"

The killer smiled stupidly. "No, sir. I reckon not."

Frank Ivy pushed his coattail behind the holster and stared at the freighter McClure. It had been a long, hot ride to Cimarron, and Frank was tired. He and Isidrio, who rode one of the McKowns' mules, went straight to Winston McClure's Freight Office. The first things he saw were the two wagons parked on the side of the adobe building, and when he peeked under the canvas tarps and saw the jail doors, blood rushed to his head.

Bald-headed Winston McClure's explanations were not assuaging his anger.

He threw the two invoices into the freighter's face.

"Those wagons should have been in E-Town two weeks ago."

McClure backed up. "I got a right to protect my investment, mister. Ian McKown owes two thousand eight hundred ninety-nine dollars and forty-seven cents. Those wagons don't go one rod farther without payment in full. And that hogleg ain't convincin' me otherwise."

Frank took a deep breath, let his anger subside, and slowly reached into his inside coat pocket and found the envelope Sam Raintree had left behind. He placed the paper on the countertop and pulled out a wad of greenbacks.

"How much again?"

McClure wet his lips. He repeated the figure, and Ivy counted out the money slowly. The freighter stared at three thousand dollars in front of him.

"You owe me one hundred dollars and fifty-three cents in change, sir," he said.

"Uh . . ."

"I'd like those wagons ready to go when I come back from grabbing a bite to eat with my friend here."

Frank waited for McClure to look up. Their eyes locked. "You understand?" he asked.

"Yes," the freighter mumbled.

"I'll expect my change then. But I'll take a receipt now."

Sandy-Hair looked at the yokes of oxen being harnessed to the freight wagons and nodded in satisfaction, saying something to the Mexican kid before turning to go into the freight office. He stopped in the dusty yard when he noticed Roland Beale standing casually, hatless and in his shirtsleeves.

"Afternoon," Beale said easily and covered the distance separating them in four steps. He smiled at the gambler. "You and the boy enjoy your grub?"

He didn't answer. Beale hadn't expected him to. Still smiling, he pointed over Sandy-Hair's shoulder toward the wagons. "Where do you think you're going with them?"

"E-Town."

The freighters stopped working, and a few ne'er-do-wells, sensing a fight, came out of the saloon. The Mexican kid stood staring, jaw agape, eyes wide. Even two old Mexicans looked up from their dominoes game in front of the mercantile. Good. Beale always enjoyed putting on a good show for a crowd.

"No," he said, drawing out the syllable and looking down at the gambler. "I don't think you are."

He let Sandy-Hair pull that shiny black revolver halfway out of the holster before swinging, slamming a right into the gambler's head. The Southerner dropped and rolled, gray hat flying one way and the pistol spinning another. As Sandy-Hair pulled himself to his knees, shaking his head, Beale walked to the revolver and kicked it. The gun flew, the freighters parted, and the revolver landed once, kicking up dust, flipped and finally rested underneath one of the wagons.

"What I'm thinking," Beale said casually, "is that those wagons stay put right where they are and you and the boy *vamanos*. You savvy?"

Sandy-Hair stood now. Beale waited for a reply.

"Go to—"

This time, Beale let him taste the left, a quick uppercut that sent the gambler sprawling in the dust.

"Mister," Beale said, helping Sandy-Hair to his feet.

"You can't lick me, and I can kill you with these." For emphasis, he followed a left to the gambler's stomach with a right to the back of his head. And Sandy-Hair was down again, face-first, pulling himself up, spitting, coughing and swearing.

"Stay down!" someone called out, but the gambler didn't listen.

Man-Killer Roland Beale sighed. "I was really hoping you wouldn't be so stupid, friend."

He blocked the punch the gambler threw, and countered with another, a glancing blow off the side of Sandy-Hair's head. The gambler backed away, still on his feet, and brought up his fists, moving them around like a would-be pugilist. Beale let the gambler take a few jabs, not even coming close, and then he sent a right that smashed Sandy-Hair's lips.

"Let's do this the easy way, friend," he said. "You don't have my reach."

Suddenly, the gambler dived, landing on his shoulder and kicking out with his fancy boots. Both heels caught Beale in the left shin, and he let out a howl and fell, reaching out for his leg. He saw the gambler's boots again, but this time he rolled, feeling the leather cut the side of his head just above the ear. Beale kept rolling until he knew he had cleared the gambler's boots, and then hopped up, testing his left leg, wiping dust and blood off his face.

Sandy-Hair also stood, fists pumping again, battered face determined.

"All right," Beale told him. "Have it your way."

He charged, blocking the gambler's swings, faked twice with the right, then sent a vicious haymaker to the man's head. Sandy-Hair rolled in the dust again, but came up quickly. Shaking his head, Beale moved in, dodging a few rights, careful not to let Sandy-Hair's boots out of his sight. The gambler got in a lucky punch to Beale's chin. Pretty solid, Beale had to admit. Swinging that hammer all day had put some meat on the boy's bones.

He heard a mix of cheers and boos, encouragement and criticism in Spanish and English. Beale blocked another punch, then assaulted Sandy-Hair's ribs. The gambler grunted, hurt, and Beale kept at it, recognizing a weakness, remembering the ribs he had busted pretty good back in E-Town. When Sandy-Hair dropped his arms to protect himself, he left his face open, and Beale responded. Once. Twice. Again. And again. The gambler dropped, and Beale stepped back to catch his breath.

The boy pleaded something in Spanish. A freighter called out, "That's enough!" Neither Beale nor Sandy-Hair listened.

Beale shook his head as the Southerner staggered, once again standing, but his eyes losing their focus. "Come on," Sandy-Hair said through busted lips, spitting out blood and sand. "Is that all you got?"

Mule-headed dunce. Beale moved quickly and pounded the gambler's head and ribs. Sandy-Hair fell hard, lay still, but then sucked in air and rolled over, crawling toward the wagons.

"The wagons stay put," Beale told him, but the gambler kept going. Sandy-Hair had no fight left in him, but he was determined to get to those wagons, to prove his point. Beale circled him, waited for the man to reach him, then picked him up and punched him hard in the stomach.

"The wagons stay put," he repeated, this time pointing a long finger at the gambler.

He watched in disbelief as Sandy-Hair sat up. The gambler's left arm stayed tight against his ribs. Blood poured from his nose and lips, and his left eye was already puffy and bruised. With a terrible groan, Sandy-Hair rose, wobbling, and staggered past Beale toward the wagons. With a curse of disbelief, Beale spun, grabbed the gambler's shoulder, jerked him around and buried his fist into the man's forehead. Sandy-Hair crashed, somersaulted, and landed spread-eagled near the first wagon.

Beale waited. His mouth fell open. The gambler reached up with his right hand, grabbed a spoke and pulled himself into a seated position.

"Don't do it," Beale said, but there Sandy-Hair was, pulling himself up, turning around and trying to climb onto the wagon.

Beale walked fast, turned the Southerner around and threw him to the ground.

"Don't make me kill you," Beale said through clenched teeth.

Yet the gambler tried to stand, breathing heavily, on his knees and elbows, summoning the strength to rise. Beale kicked him in the stomach, watched the gambler roll over, and he moved in. He would have to kill this man. He couldn't see any way around it. The fool should be unconscious or dead already.

"No!" Beale heard the loud cry, saw the Mexican boy sailing at him. Beale grabbed the boy's dirty shirt and flung him aside. When the boy climbed to his feet and charged again, Beale cursed his luck. He let the boy sail into him, then took the kid by his throat and lifted him off the ground. The boy's eyes bulged. He kicked, swung widely, fought for breath. Beale knew he would have to kill the kid, too.

"*Señor, por favor*, release my son."

Turning slightly, Man-Killer Roland Beale saw a white-haired Mexican peasant with scraggly mustache and goatee. The man looked poorer than dirt, but he held an ancient rifle pointed directly at Beale's face. Just behind the peasant stood a half-dozen other Mexicans. They didn't wield firearms like that old flintlock, but two had pitchforks, one a whip, and the other two shovels.

Beale lowered the Mexican kid to the ground.

"*Bueno*," the old relic said. "*Por favor, vamanos.* Or my sons and I shall be forced to kill you this afternoon."

Silently, Beale walked past the Mexicans, picked up his hat and coat that he had left on a hitching post before the fight and walked away. The Major wouldn't like this, but right now Roland Beale didn't care what the Major liked or thought. He turned only once as he headed for the livery. The Mexican boy was talking excitedly, gesturing frantically, to the old man, and Sandy-Hair, dazed and half-dead, unaware that the fight had ended, that Beale was gone, leaned against the wagon, trying to climb into the seat.

Chapter Nineteen

Isidrio Adán Pascual Silvestre tried to explain everything to his father, but so much had happened, so quickly. He heard *Señor* Frank mumble something and groan, and as Isidrio turned he saw the gambler fall to the ground once more and roll over near the wagon wheel. This time, *Señor* Frank did not get back up.

He sprinted toward the man, whose eye that was not swollen shut opened and fluttered as Isidrio knelt. The breaths of the gambler were ragged, but at least he still lived. Blood streamed from his mangled lips and nose, but still he managed to swallow and speak: "Isidrio, get these wagons to McKown."

"Do not worry, *señor*," Isidrio's father said behind him. "My son will see that your wish is granted."

Isidrio looked at his father, who with a nod com-

151

manded Isidrio's brothers to help. Miguel, the oldest, squatted over *Señor* Frank, now unconscious, and began checking the man's many injuries. Pedro filled his sombrero with water from the trough in front of the freight office and carried it to them. Isidrio began washing the gambler's face, while the other brothers stood around, waiting for a command from their father.

"This gringo should be dead," Miguel said. "I believe one of his ribs has put a hole in a lung."

"He cannot die!" Isidrio exclaimed.

He felt his father's hand on his shoulder. "He will not die, Isidrio. Where is the doctor?"

Miguel snorted. "The drunk *gringo*? In a saloon. Which one I do not know."

"Then we must take him to your mother. As soon as he is able to travel, we will put him in a cart and bring him to Elizabethtown."

Isidrio nodded. His father had always been a wise man. But the gambler had entrusted Isidrio with a job, and Isidrio could not disappoint *Señor* Frank.

"As soon as you can, you must bring him to the courthouse and jail being built there," Isidrio said. "I must make sure these wagons reach *Señor* McKown."

"You have not returned home, Little One?" Pedro asked.

"No, my brother. I have a job in Elizabethtown. I am a carpenter."

His father nodded. "It is an honorable profession." He looked away. "You are leaving with the wagons today?"

"*Sí, papa.*"

"Very well. But not before you kiss your mother and show her how much you have grown."

Isidrio stood beside his father, watching his brothers gently carry the gambler away. The crowd that had gathered to watch the senseless brawl between *Señor* Frank and *el gigante negro* had disappeared into the saloons, seeking shelter from the relentless heat. But one old Mexican man remained. Isidrio recognized him as one of the domino players who had wondered what would become of the poor boy when Isidrio left Cimarron.

"Nicanor Silvestre, *mi amigo*," the *viejo* said, addressing Isidrio's father. "Who is this boy to whom you are talking? He looks familiar."

His father smiled. "Boy? I see no boy, Enrique. But this *man*—he is my son, Isidrio Adán Pascual Silvestre, a carpenter in Elizabethtown."

Fresh bottle in his hand, James McKown wandered down Front Street on his way back to his claim when he saw the large wagons being unloaded at his father's construction site. That stopped him in his boots. Openmouthed, he stared for a full minute before slipping the whiskey into his coat pocket and crossed the street.

"What's going on?" he asked Conall.

"Supplies got here," his brother answered. "No thanks to you."

"What does that mean?" James tried to fake a belligerent tone, but doubted if he succeeded. They knew he had sold them out to those thugs. He should have known better, should have lied to those killers. But he had been a coward. Again. Trying to protect himself instead of his family.

His father stepped from behind a wagon to answer James's question. "You know, James," he said bitterly.

He nodded at the lump in James's coat. "Buy some courage this afternoon?"

"I don't know what you mean."

Old Iron-Headed Ian exploded, a savage lashing that caused James to step backward. "Don't play us for fools, boy!" he shouted. "I should have known not to tell you anything when you started being so friendly after all these months."

"Papa—"

"No! Do not Papa me. Frank Ivy is stove-up down in Cimarron, because of you. To my way of thinking, you should be one of the first customers in this jail. You sold us out, boy. For what? Money? To get even with me? *Answer me!*"

James swallowed, staring at his father and brother. Old Iron-Headed Ian suddenly looked ancient, not the old warhorse he had known and feared for so many years. James's answer was soft, barely a whisper: "I don't know why."

Why? Because he feared the two men who had threatened him? Partly. It hadn't been because of the money. Or was Papa right? Had he done it to get even with his own family?

Shaking his head, his father went on, quieter now: "For years now, I thought I had been too hard on you, James. But now I know that I wasn't hard enough. Well, I hope they paid you well, boy. Go back to your claim. It's all yours now. You don't have to worry about me sending your sister to get our share. I don't want any part of it. I don't want any part of you."

James blinked. "Papa . . ."

"I have two sons now. One's Conall. The other is William up in the cemetery."

He turned, went back to help unload the wagons. Conall left him, too.

"You think you're so high and mighty! You think this building will bring justice to this miserable town? Well, it won't. It won't bring William back either! It never had anything to do with Will anyhow, Papa. It was always about you. Well, I don't need you. I don't want you. None of you. You can all . . ."

He realized he had been yelling, saw that no one listened to him, not even the Mexican freighters. Only that young Mexican carpenter, Isidrio, stared at him, and pretty soon he went back to work. James stood for a while hoping Alice would come to him, but she didn't. He couldn't blame her, or them. Slowly, he turned and moved down the street, partly in a daze. His hand found the whiskey, and he withdrew it, pulled out the cork with his teeth, tilted the bottle up, and drank.

"How do you feel?" she asked.

"How do I look?" came Frank's answer.

He was sitting up, leaning against the wall in what would become the town marshal's office. Isidrio's father and brothers had brought Ivy from Cimarron in an ox-pulled cart, his ribs and other injuries bandaged, his face bruised and cut, his knuckles skinned. That had been a week ago. He still looked awful, but she smiled and lied, "You're the handsomest man I've seen in ages."

The laugh caused him to wince, and he reached for his ribs. "I'm not earning my keep around here," he said. "I think your father might fire me pretty soon."

"He might. I don't think you'll be climbing any ladders or lifting jail-cell doors anytime soon. I'm not even sure you can deal cards in your present condition." She paused. "We'll be finished soon."

He looked at her, his smile gone. "And then what?"

She shrugged. "I really don't know. Papa hasn't said anything. I thought we might stay here, but . . ."

"Will *you* stay?"

"I don't know. It's a beautiful place. Papa, though, he gets the itch to travel, see the country. And with what happened to William and . . . James . . . he might . . ." She couldn't finish.

"What do you want, Alice?" he asked.

She looked away. "I've always gone with Papa. Well, I'd best get back to work. Holler if you need anything."

She stood in the doorway when Frank called out her name. She wet her lips before she turned, hoping her tears didn't start rolling down her face.

"If I were to ask you . . . I mean, not as a gambler . . . I . . . I can get some kind of work. Well, I mean I have enough money for a couple to start a new life together . . . Do you think . . . is your place always going to be with your father? What I'm saying, Alice, is that . . . well . . . if I were to ask you . . ."

She felt herself smiling again. Frank Ivy had always been so sure of himself, but now he acted like a schoolboy, nervous, unable to blurt out what he really wanted to ask.

"You'll have to ask me, Frank," she said.

"Yeah," he answered after a minute. "I just haven't done it before."

"You're doing fine."

She could hear her heart pounding now, waiting, wanting for him to ask her. Yet before he could, Conall was calling for her and her father to hurry up outside. She could have stayed, made Papa and Conall wait, but maybe a little time would help Frank decide how he should propose.

"I'll be back, Frank," she said, turning. "And I hope you know what I'll say."

The freighter cut the string and pulled back the tarp, revealing the tombstone.

WILLIAM WALLACE McKOWN
BORN IN CAMDEN, SOUTH CAROLINA
MARCH 12, 1848
MURDERED IN ELIZABETHTOWN, NEW MEXICO TY.
MAY 30, 1869

Alice reached out to take her father's hand. She had almost forgotten about the tombstone, forgotten those horrible memories. May 30. How long ago did that seem now. The freighter asked something, and Papa mumbled an answer. Conall helped the man unload the heavy marble, while Papa took a seat on a camp stool. He didn't say anything until long after the freighter had left and she and Conall stood at his side.

"You want me to take it up to the cemetery, Father?" Conall asked. "Put it up?"

"That's good," he answered, rubbing his right arm, not looking up.

"I'll take Isidrio to help," Conall said. "We'll be back soon. You just rest."

She sat beside Papa as her brother hitched the team and loaded the tombstone. She chatted idly about anything that came into her head, wanting to take Papa's mind off the tombstone, off William, off everything. Finally, sensing the uselessness of that tactic, she said maybe they could go up Sunday morning to visit William, to see how good the tombstone looked.

"It is beautiful," she said, although she really found it cold as the chiseled marble. "William would be proud of you, Papa. I'm proud of you, too."

He looked at her with hollow eyes. She had never seen him cry before, but tears streamed down his cheeks, and he shook his head. "James was right, Alice," he said, the first time he had mentioned her brother's name in weeks. "This never was about William. It was all about me. My vanity. My selfishness. I never was much of a father. I'm sorry about that. And the law will never come to this place. The people here don't want it. What was I thinking?"

Ian McKown rose, hammer in hand, staring at the two-story building. "Alice," he said, "that Ivy fellow can take care of you, better than me."

"Papa . . ."

He sighed. "I'd best get back to work," he said, wiping his eyes. She sat still, aware of her own tears, and watched him take a dozen steps before he dropped the hammer and toppled like a falling pine.

Chapter Twenty

Major Judd Howard couldn't believe his luck. Laughing until his sides hurt, he spun around in his leather chair and poured himself a drink. "This is a cause to celebrate," he said, still so amused that he splashed a good bit of the cheap hooch onto the table and floor. "Anyone care to join me?" he asked as he sent the chair spinning around to face his hired assassins.

King Stevens, Deke Goss and Man-Killer Roland Beale politely declined his offer.

Howard took a healthy swallow and slid the glass on his desk. "So what exactly happened? Anyone know?"

The marshal shrugged. "Old man's pump broke, least that's what everybody's saying."

"Heart attack, eh?"

"Yes sir."

He drank some more.

Ian McKown was dead.

What that probably meant was that that unrecon-structed Reb's family—boils on his neck all summer—would pack up and move to warmer climes, taking that idiot Mexican boy and stubborn gambler with them. And the Elizabethtown Courthouse and Jail would be left for the good mayor and marshal of E-Town.

"Heart attack!" Howard laughed and drank again. They had tried to burn the fool out, threaten him, turned his own son against him, and run off as many of his hired hands as they could. Two freighters had been killed on McKown's account. Not only that, Deke Goss had murdered the secesh's youngest son. All of that work, all of that sweat, and what had hap-pened in the end?

"God's on our side, gentlemen," Howard said gid-dily. "God is on our side."

Deke Goss showed off his brown teeth in a stupid grin. "What you want us to do next, Major?"

"Oh, I'm not the Prince of Darkness, Goss. We'll let the good Reb be buried properly, let the McKowns clear out of the valley. Then we'll move into our new home and get back to work. I'm thinking it's high time we took care of that newspaper editor. His scathing editorials and dumb news stories are beginning to an-noy me."

Man-Killer Beale straightened and asked, "What if the McKowns stay put?"

Howard scratched his chin. "What the Sam Hill has gotten into you, Beale? You've been acting like a yellow-bellied Johnny Reb since you botched that job down in Cimarron."

"I'm just not convinced the McKowns will leave, Major," he said.

"Oh, they'll run all right, Beale. Their pappy was the only one keeping them together. They'll run. We'll be rid of them in no time, and then we'll be rid of *The Moreno Lantern*, and we'll get back to business."

It hurt to walk, but Frank Ivy gritted his teeth and led his palomino mare, draped in black, behind the wagon hauling Ian McKown's coffin. He saw Alice leaning against Conall's shoulder as her big brother flicked the reins and drove the wagon up Front Street on the way to the cemetery. Frank hoped he could climb the steep hill without collapsing.

Behind him walked young Isidrio, carrying a handful of New Mexico sunflowers, and then came the others: the merchant Lobenstein, the newspaper editor Ferguson, a few other men and women Frank didn't know. A mighty small turnout for a fine man.

He still couldn't believe the old man was gone. He could still hear Alice's scream. Ivy had pulled himself up, grabbed his Dance revolver and stumbled outside to find Alice on the ground, cradling her father's head in her lap, wailing, the wind blowing her hair, the old man pale, mouth open, eyes closed. Dead. He sank to his knees beside Alice, and let her cry on his shoulder. Frank hadn't known how to propose to her just minutes ago, and he certainly didn't know what to say now, so he let her cry, held her tight against him despite his sore ribs, and waited for Conall and Isidrio to return.

Conall had built the coffin himself, and they had

washed Ian's face, put on his best coat, and laid him in the pine box along with his hammer and the blueprints for the courthouse, which would be finished within the week. Frank wished the old man could have lived that much longer.

As the procession marched past the Moreno Hotel, two men stepped off the boardwalk, newspapers in their hands, and dropped in line silently, heads bowed, hats off. Mr. Lobenstein's wife left the mercantile, hanging up a "Closed" sign, and took her place beside the merchant. Other men and women soon took their place, many of them dressed in black and those without black hats or coats wearing black scarves.

He had thought too harshly of the people of E-Town. Halfway up the hill, he paused to catch his breath and turned. A line of mourners stretched all the way down the hill, winding along Front Street and disappearing beyond the Elkhorn Saloon.

Judd Howard had been in a pretty good mood, standing underneath the awning to pay his last respects to Mr. Ian McKown, smoking a cigar and nodding politely at the big oaf and his plain sister, both of them ignoring him, as they carried their dead daddy to feed the worms up that hill.

His mood quickly soured, though, as more and more people joined the funeral throng. It was Saturday, and payday, but even the Montezuma Bar and Club Rooms, the Miner's Inn and the Senate had closed their doors. So had all of the other businesses not owned and operated by Major Judd Howard. The sawmills were quiet. No pounding of hammer against anvil came from Damaso's Livery. The only noise seemed to be hundreds, maybe even thousands, of feet along Front Street and the shutting of doors.

"Major?"

Howard turned, saw King Stevens holding the latest edition of *The Moreno Lantern*. He snatched the paper from the marshal and saw the bold headline on the right-hand corner at the top of the page. "E-Town Mourns Its Greatest Loss." He read the story.

Mr. Ian McKown, carpenter, has gone to Glory, far from the Hades that seems to be the Moreno Valley, far from the pain.

A few months ago, I promised not to editorialize in my news stories, but now I must break that promise. I must say how I feel, how I hope many of us feel, at the passing of Mr. McKown.

I am ashamed.

I am ashamed that I did not take a stronger stand supporting Mr. McKown's dream of bringing law and order to E-Town. I am a coward. I have spent much ink and paper demanding that our officials, "Mayor" Howard and "Marshal" Stevens, do more, work harder. But I will not soil this story by mentioning the names of those fiends anymore in this bit of prose.

Mr. McKown lost a son to the men purported to be responsible for overseeing justice in E-Town. While we watched—while many of you laughed—the carpenter went to work to build a dream, a jail and courthouse. He thought, I think, that through his efforts, the good men and women of this community would back him, support him, defend him and help him. He thought we wanted justice. He thought we would take up for ourselves at last and drive the vermin from the valley.

He was wrong, of course. And he died.

So all of us—myself included—should feel shame for our cowardice.

When I first arrived in this beautiful valley, E-Town had a population of six thousand. Today, many of those have departed for warmer climes. I estimate we have a population of three thousand now, and by winter that number will likely be no more than one thousand. But how many of those "snowbirds" will return next spring and summer to a place that has little semblance of law or humanity? If we want to make E-Town a decent town, we still have a chance. Yes, we can still live up to the late Mr. McKown's ideals.

Today is not the time for us to act, but act we must—against evil tyranny and injustice—soon. Today is the day for us to honor Mr. McKown's memory. This afternoon, you'll find me paying my final respects, a last tribute to a great man with a great dream.

If you are not too ashamed, I hope you will join me.

Tomorrow, though, we must strike back.

Viva Ian McKown!

Howard ripped the pages and tossed them into the air, swearing, spitting out his five-cent cigar. "Have Beale break Mr. Jonathan Ferguson's hands. Now."

"Where is Man-Killer?" the lawman asked.

"I don't know," Howard began, but then he saw the tremendous pugilist, marching at the rear of the funeral procession, hat in hand.

* * *

James McKown waited until the crowd dispersed. He had not expected that many people to attend Old Iron-Headed Ian's funeral. He stood beside the grove of trees, watched, and tried to listen, although the circuit preacher's words were lost on him. In many ways, he was glad to see so many E-Town residents show up, not only because his father deserved it, but because he didn't want Conall and Alice to see him.

Well, they hadn't, and now he stood alone, chilled by the hard wind, and stared at the wooden cross Conall had nailed together and on it carved:

IAN MCKOWN
1809–1869

He wondered at the number of people who had attended the funeral, not leaving until the coffin had been lowered, the grave covered, and Conall, Alice, Ivy and Isidrio had left.

Papa rested beside Will's grave, James's brother's marble monument dwarfing the pine cross made of scraps from the courthouse job. But Papa would have wanted that. James didn't remember walking, but soon he found himself standing at the foot of Papa's grave, staring at the sunflowers the Mexican boy must have put there.

Clenching the brim of his hat tightly at his waist, James said, "Papa . . ." And then the dam broke.

He fell to his knees, dropping his hat which the wind carried away, and cried. He wanted the tears and pangs to stop, but they wouldn't, and he fell forward on the fresh mound of dirt and buried his hands in the clod. He hadn't expected this, not the tears, certainly not the awful pain.

"Papa!" he shouted. "Oh, Papa, I failed you. I'm so sorry." The sobs became choking, like short breaths from a struggling steam engine, and he rolled over, rising to his knees, the wind burning his face. "I'll do everything I can to make it up to you, Papa," he said. "You don't have to forgive me. I don't deserve it. But Papa . . ."

He knew then why he hurt so much. For so long, James had thought he had hated his father, and now he knew he had loved him.

Only it was too late to tell him.

Chapter Twenty-one

She opened the front door to the courthouse and screamed, stepping back, bringing both hands to her mouth. Frank pushed her aside, grabbed the Barrett's Combination Roller Gauge leaning against the wall, and stepped inside, wielding the metal tool as if it were a nightstick. It wasn't, and weighing less than a pound, it was a poor choice for a weapon, but it was all Frank had.

"Go ahead," the voice from the shadows drawled. "Whup the tar outta me. I deserve it."

Ivy lowered the gauge, recognizing the thick Texas accent before Sam Raintree stepped into the light.

"The Yankee sawbones at Fort Union did a fair job of patchin' me up," Sam was saying, sitting on the bottom of the staircase, sipping Conall's coffee. Frank leaned against the doorjamb, drinking coffee himself while taking in the aroma of sawdust. To his right sat Alice, Conall and Isidrio.

"That ol' colored boy put a hurt on me somethin' good. So it took a spell for me to leave Fort Union. Well, I was all set to ride east to Abilene, and I started out that way. But the farther I rode, the more it galled me. I ain't never run from no fight. So I told myself, 'Sam, you've let your only friend down, let down Mr. McKown, too.' " He shook his head and swore. "I knowed how much this buildin' meant to y'all, knowed it never had a thing to do with that bet as far as Frank was concerned. So I turned my hoss around and headed back here. Wish I coulda made it sooner. Your daddy might be still alive."

Alice shook her head. "It wasn't your fault, Sam. It was Papa's heart, not Mayor Howard, not anything you did."

"Well, I'm here to help. Not much left to do, but I'm here."

Conall McKown, suddenly looking and sounding just like the old man, walked over and extended his massive hand toward the Texan. "We're proud to have you back, Sam. Mighty proud."

Four whiskeys hadn't eased Judd Howard's anger that Sunday afternoon. He rubbed the stump of his arm and swore, kicked a wastebasket across the Elkhorn's office and asked Man-Killer Roland Beale: "Just what did you think you were doing, Beale, paying your last respects?"

"Something like that, Major."

The fact that the boxer had joined the funeral procession didn't bother Howard that much. The more he thought about it, the more he wished he had fallen in line to take off his hat and sing some hymn on that hilltop. Then, when everyone had left, he could have spit on Ian McKown's grave and laughed. But that Ferguson had stirred up the crowd with his blistering article, and if *The Moreno Lantern* printed next week, Major Howard might find his support, or rather the town's tolerance, blowing away. Deke Goss and the half-breed Gideon would be seeing that that didn't happen, but Howard had to strike harder, make the three thousand people in E-Town remember that Judd Howard, mayor and major, still ruled the Moreno Valley.

Next, King Stevens brought him more bad news. The Texan whom Beale had pounded into the Front Street dirt was back with the McKowns. Howard had underestimated everyone involved: the secessionist McKown and his family, the two gamblers Ivy and Raintree, and that fool journalist Ferguson.

Deke Goss rapped lightly on the door. Now what? Howard thought, and told the dwarf to come on in. The Missourian smiled and said, "That newspaperman ain't gonna be writin' nothin' for a while, Major. Gideon and me broke this printin' press to smithereens. And then we broke both of his hands."

King Stevens began to smile, and Howard felt the whiskey warming him, putting him—finally—in a better mood. Until he saw Beale shaking his head.

"What is it now, Beale?" he snapped.

"Just that I'm not sure beating up Ferguson and ransacking his office were smart."

"How dare you question me!" he roared. Howard could take a lot of things, but . . .

"Hear me out, Major," Beale went on. "Half the town turned out for McKown's funeral, mostly on account of what that newspaper editor wrote. So now you beat him up, ruin his press, what do you think the folks in the valley will be saying? You stoke up a fire till it's red hot, well, it's not to smart to throw coal oil on it right afterward."

Howard tried to slow his breathing and heartbeat. Deke Goss looked stupidly, not knowing what to say or do.

"Maybe he's got a point, Major," Stevens said. "But if we don't regain control, we might have a hard time fighting off a party with a bunch of tar and feathers."

"Or a rope," Beale added.

Sinking into his chair, Howard braced his chin in his hand. How could he have let things spin out of control so quickly? And what could he do to stop it before he found himself being escorted to the territorial prison in Santa Fe? Or lynched, as he had ordered so many people—guilty and innocent—strung up in the valley?

"You want my suggestion, Major?" Stevens asked.

"Go on," he said quietly.

"A show of force can take the starch out of a lynch mob. I think it's time the Moreno Valley Vigilante Committee showed who's top rooster in E-Town. We get a bunch of the boys together and we hang that Texas gambler."

"For what?"

"Well, maybe I've concluded that he was responsible for the death of them two freighters earlier this summer in the Palisades." Stevens grinned slightly. "We can try to serve him a warrant. And them McKowns. Harboring a killer is a serious crime."

"They'll fight," Beale said.

"I know," Stevens went on. "But who's gonna be fighting us? A carpenter, two gamblers, a Mex boy and a gal? Against the Vigilante Committee? We'll put a torch to that courthouse to smoke them out. Then we'll display the dead bodies in front of Lobenstein's mercantile to show what we do to lawbreakers."

Deke Goss shook his head. "I don't know, King. Killin' a woman and a boy, that . . ."

"Shows we are serious," Howard interjected. He opened the top desk drawer, pulled out the Walking Beam revolver and stood so quickly that the leather chair tipped over backward and crashed on the floor. "And not ones to be trifled with. Round up as many boys as you can, King. Let's serve your arrest warrant first thing tomorrow morn."

Isidrio stepped outside to fetch more crown molding. He found it strange that just two days after the McKowns had buried their father, they were back at work. If his own father were to die, he did not think he could carry on for at least a week. But these people, his friends, were strong, so Isidrio, even though he missed *Señor* McKown greatly, would be strong with them.

He placed his right sandal on the first step leading off the big porch and stopped. Many *gringos* surrounded the courthouse. At first, he thought they came to bring food or express sympathy at the passing of *Señor* McKown, but one of them raised a rifle, and Isidrio opened his mouth in horror. He wanted to scream or at least say a prayer to the Virgin Mary, but no words sounded.

"Isidrio?" The voice, that of *Señor* Conall, came

from behind. Isidrio heard the footsteps of the big carpenter, and the dark muzzle of the rifle rose slightly. *Señor* Conall suddenly shouted, "Isidrio! Get down!" And the rifle boomed.

He turned now, tripping on the step and falling onto the porch, splinters burying themselves into his small hands. Another rifle shot thundered, and Isidrio closed his eyes. He felt someone crush his wrists, and suddenly, as bullets whined over his ears and dug into the frame building, he was dragged across the porch and tossed inside like a sack of *frijoles*. The door slammed shut, only to be peppered by bullets, and Isidrio opened his eyes. *Señor* Conall was kneeling over him, blood dripping down the man's stocky left arm.

"Are you all right, boy?" the carpenter asked as gunshots exploded outside.

"*Sí*," Isidrio answered. Footsteps and excited voices sounded all around him. Glass in windows shattered. Lead thumped the solid walls. *Señor* Conall pointed his bloody arm toward a corner, near one of the heaters they had put in just last week. "Get over there, Isidrio, and keep your head down!"

Frank Ivy squeezed into a corner, holding the Dance .44 in his right hand. He motioned Alice to take cover beside Isidrio, and looked around for McKown and Raintree. The burly carpenter sat on the floor and wrapped a bandana around his right forearm. He couldn't find Sam, then remembered that the Texan had been working upstairs.

"Sam?" he shouted above the noise of musketry.

"Yeah!"

He took a short breath of relief. Raintree was still alive.

The Texan yelled: "Looks like about a dozen or more men, Frank! And all I got is my Colt. What about you?"

"My revolver. Rifle's in McKown's tent outside."

"No more guns?"

Ivy shook his head, realized the stupidity of that, and called out, "No."

Sam Raintree responded with an oath. "Two pistols ain't gonna stop them boys, Frank. I only got four rounds left, iffen nothin' misfires. You?"

Ivy hadn't fired. "Five," he said, suddenly wishing he never bought into the safety idea that you should keep an empty chamber under the hammer.

The Texan swore again.

Almost as quickly as it had started, the cannonade outside subsided, replaced by a wiry voice: "This is Marshal King Stevens. Come out with your hands up, or we'll burn you out."

Frank wet his lips. "What's the charge?" he asked, trying to buy some time.

"That Texan killed those two freighters this summer. He's wanted for two murders, and you all are aiding him. Make it easy on yourselves."

Yeah, Frank thought, to be shot trying to escape.

"*Señor* Frank!"

Ivy turned, saw Isidrio sticking his head above the corner window. "Get down!" he snapped, and the boy dropped just as a rifle slug tore through the windowsill and sang off the stovepipe.

The boy, eyes wide, now hugged tightly by Alice, said, "I saw a man! He is running around the side of the house! He carries a torch!"

His ribs hurt. The gun felt heavy in his hand, useless. He had no shot at the man on the other side of the house.

"It's gonna get hot in there mighty soon!" Stevens yelled. "Cover him, boys!"

Gunfire resumed.

Frank dropped to his hands and knees and crawled across the floor, through the doorway that led to the foyer. Safe, at least he hoped so, from the volleys splintering the front of the building, he moved to the side door, gripped the knob and jerked.

He had come to town expecting to die, a note addressed to Alice, explaining everything, stuck in his trouser pocket. Not suicide. Well, not quite. No, James McKown would walk into the Elkhorn Saloon, head up the stairs, kick open the door and shoot Judd Howard as many times as he could. And then, more than likely, one of the major's killers would fill James's body full of lead.

He cut through the forest to see the courthouse and jail one last time. Then he heard the gunfire.

It took a full minute to understand what was happening. Jerking the Manhattan revolver from his waistband, James ran, dodging the trees and forests, sweating. He almost didn't see the man leaning against the pine until it was too late. The guy in the plaid britches and brocade vest spun around, rifle in hand, and opened his mouth as if to scream. James recognized the face, knew this was the gambler who had hurt Alice, saw the man—Rowley, that was his name—bring up the Enfield.

James didn't remember pulling the trigger, but he saw the rifle falling and Rowley being driven back, eyes and mouth still open. James didn't bother to look back. On he ran until he cleared the trees as the dark-haired half-breed ran toward the building with a torch in his left hand and a shiny rifle in his right.

He yelled something, not sure what, and moved on, like in a dream, slow, strange, unreal. The breed turned around, dropped the torch and brought the rifle up to his shoulder, jerking hard on the lever, cursing. James pulled the trigger again. Cocked the hammer. Fired once more. He knew he had missed both times, and now the killer had his rifle ready. The door opened, and the breed spun around, hurrying a shot that went high and wide.

The gambler, Frank Ivy, stepped outside, fired. James shot also, and the breed dropped to his knees, made the sign of the cross, and pitched forward. Still James ran, now aware of bullets screaming over his head and pounding the dirt all around him. Ivy was shouting something. James couldn't quite understand. Ivy spun, ducked, fired again, turned back, pointed his revolver barrel at the dead half-breed.

"The rifle!" his mouth formed. "Get the rifle!"

James understood. He shifted the Manhattan into his left hand, and scooped up the breed's rifle. Still he ran. And then he felt the hard punch in his back, driving him to his knees, ten yards from the steps. Ivy started to climb down the steps, but a bullet knocked off the heel on the gambler's left boot, and he crashed hard. Another bullet splintered the pine column just above Ivy's head.

James couldn't run. Couldn't hear. Couldn't feel anything. He felt another bullet slam into his side. He looked down, still on his knees, saw the Manhattan in his left hand, the lever-action rifle in his right. He felt himself falling, but pitched the rifle as hard as he could toward Frank Ivy, now scrambling back inside as bullets tore the wood all around him.

James crashed into the dirt, felt another bullet burn his right leg. Lifting his head, he moved the revolver to his right hand as another bullet dug into his side, just below the ribs. He felt the blood forming in his mouth, and his head, too heavy, dropped. He realized he had landed in a pile of sawdust. He thought of his father, knowing he had failed Old Iron-Headed Ian once again.

Chapter Twenty-two

Frank grimaced and barked out a curse as a bullet tore through his left hand. Another clipped his collar. He flattened himself, popped off a useless shot and saw the Henry rifle sailing end over end, landing on the doorsteps. James McKown had fallen face down and no longer moved. Ivy sat up quickly, fired until the Dance emptied, pitched the revolver away and gripped the barrel of the Henry. He stood, felt another bullet cut a furrow across his back as he turned and dived back into the doorway, his chest exploding in agony as he hit the wood floor, ribs shooting pain throughout his chest. Still he rolled over, kicked shut the door and began crawling on his back toward the front office.

He hugged his ribs as if to hold his chest together

and attempted to call out to Sam that he had a rifle. Alice suddenly knelt over him, trying to help him, and big Conall jerked the Henry from his grip and disappeared into the front office.

Ivy looked into Alice's eyes.

"It was James," he said.

She turned, ashen, heading for the door, but his right hand shot out and snatched her wrist.

"No!" he shouted. "There's nothing you can do for him!"

The door kicked open, and Frank reached for a gun, realized he had none—nothing, no weapon—and saw the bantam killer named Goss and Marshal King Stevens fill the doorway. He wasn't quite sure of what happened next.

One second the little assassin was leveling his revolver at Frank's chest, and the next his own shirt front erupted crimson and he fell outside. King Stevens ducked, aimed up the staircase and fired. Frank turned, saw Sam Raintree rolling halfway down the stairs, leaving a trail of blood. He knew then that the Texan had killed Goss before Stevens had shot him. Frank heard the roar of the Henry in the other room— Conall McKown had no idea what was going on in the foyer behind him—and realized as the marshal lowered his Navy revolver and thumbed back the hammer that he and Alice would die right now.

But just as those thoughts flashed through Frank Ivy's mind, King Stevens gasped and wheeled around, sinking to the floor with a sharp two-by-four stake protruding from his back, the doorway suddenly blocked by a ducking Man-Killer Roland Beale. Stevens aimed his revolver at the black boxer and pulled the trigger.

The bullet popped Beale dead-center, but he ignored the wound. Stevens fired again. Again. And next the marshal and killer of Elizabethtown screamed, dropping his gun as Man-killer Roland Beale reared back and sent a crushing right to Stevens's head. The killer spun around on his knees, eyes no longer seeing, and fell forward.

Roland Beale, his white shirt covered with blood, turned and stepped outside into the maelstrom.

Judd Howard had emptied the Whitney and grabbed a .44 Colt. He hadn't lost his arm hiding behind some wagon back at Glorieta, and he wasn't going to hide now. He waited until the rifle fire from the courthouse stopped before taking off after King Stevens, and was about to pick up the torch Stevens, Goss and Beale had ignored—only to stop when a bloodied Man-Killer stepped out of the building and hobbled down the steps.

The boxer started for Howard. At first, the major didn't know what to do. He heard shouts of his men out front screaming and pointing down Front Street. Two of them sprang for their horses and spurred them down the Cimarron Road. Howard lowered the revolver and looked. He couldn't believe it.

It looked like two-thirds of E-Town's populace came marching down the street, wielding guns, pitchforks, shovels, pickaxes, rifles, shotguns, revolvers, anything, shouting angrily, gesturing wildly, shooting or even throwing rocks at what was left of the Moreno Valley Vigilante Committee. He recognized the leaders of the group—that reckless journalist Ferguson, his broken hands wrapped in white linen; Captain William

Moore, armed with a shotgun; even that timid little merchant Lobenstein.

Howard's men were running. And Howard knew he should run, too. He turned, only to see a flash and feel a staggering blow that sent him flying into the yard. He knew his jaw had been broken, but he sat up, ignoring the pain, and watched Roland Beale come forward, to finish the job. Surprised to find the .44 still in his grip, Howard raised the Army Colt and pumped four shots into the boxer's stomach as quick as he could cock and fire. Yet the leviathan came on. Howard pulled himself to his feet, and shot again. This time, Man-Killer Roland Beale sank to his knees, and fell on his side.

He wanted to shout, but couldn't. Where was Stevens? Rowley? The others? He saw the lifeless bodies of Deke Goss and Gideon, of the stupid McKown boy. A bullet whined over his head, and Howard looked behind him, saw the crowd of Moreno Valley residents after him. Howard panicked. He clipped off another shot, turned back, saw Jeff Rowley's pinto tethered to a pine.

Judd Howard ran, leaping over the form of Beale, heading for his horse. The carpenter boy, James McKown, rolled over, still alive after all, and Howard saw the revolver in the idiot's hand, saw the muzzle flash, and then he saw no more.

Helped by Isidrio, Frank Ivy limped outside, stunned, in pain, amazed to still be alive, trying to figure out what had happened. A large group of men had thrown ropes around what was left of Major Howard's men, some of them screaming for a necktie party, others cautioning against that form of justice.

Conall stood over Alice, who cradled James's bloody body in her lap, crying again. The newspaper editor, merchant Lobenstein, Captain Moore and many others soon gathered around the McKowns, hats in hand, mumbling apologies for taking action too late.

Frank looked down at Howard, a bullet in his forehead, and moved on to the giant boxer, who for some reason had killed King Stevens and saved Frank's life. And Alice's. It hurt to bend, but Ivy sank to his knees beside the dying pugilist. He'd never understand what made Beale turn sides. He'd never be able to thank the boxer.

A shadow crossed his face. Ivy looked up to find Sam Raintree clutching a bloody left shoulder, scowling in pain. Isidrio, still shaking, went over to the Texan. "You come," the boy told the gambler. "You sit and rest." And he helped Raintree to the bullet-riddled front porch.

A mumble came from Beale, and Frank looked down at the man.

"Mister?" Ivy began, but couldn't think of anything else to say.

The boxer smiled. "My name is John Adams Wilson," he said. "And I've never felt better in my life."

Then he died.

It took almost all of his strength to stand, but Frank made it, and limped to the front of the building, looking at the shattered window panes, the walls and doors perforated with bullet holes, some parts splintered into near oblivion. But one thing, miraculously, hadn't been touched: the sign Alice had painted after the funeral and hung above the door.

Elizabethtown Courthouse and Jail
Established 1869
In Memory of Ian and William McKown

Chapter Twenty-three

"Wish you'd stay," Sam Raintree said, left arm in a sling and the five-point star stamped MARSHAL pinned on his shirt front.

Frank Ivy, his own left hand bandaged, shook his head. "Alice lost two brothers and her father here, Sam. Too many bad memories."

"Yeah, pard. I understand. Ain't gonna be the same in these parts without you, though. Where you headed?"

A cool breeze kicked in, and Ivy turned up his collar. The windows in the courthouse had been boarded up, waiting for replacement glass to arrive, and the leaves on the aspens blazed with colors. Soon the winds would be bitterly cold, and the verdant valley Frank and Sam had seen when they first arrived in E-

Town would be covered in snow. Jon Ferguson had been right. Already, the town's population had dwindled, many of the rough-hewn cabins and lean-tos abandoned, and the canvas tents packed away as miners and mining-camp parasites moved down from the high country.

After burying brother James beside William and Ian, Conall McKown had packed up his wagon and joined the exodus, carrying young Isidrio Silvestre with him (with the blessing of the boy's family in Cimarron), headed for Denver City up in Colorado Territory to hang up a shingle as McKown-Silvestre Company, General Contractors. Alice kissed her brother and the Mexican boy and smiled, wishing them luck. She had stayed behind, with Frank.

He hadn't asked her that question, but he—and she, also—knew that he would. Right now, it seemed too soon after so much violence. They'd wait until they were long gone from the Moreno Valley. And then he'd ask her to marry him. And she, by God's grace, would say yes.

Frank realized he had been lost in thought, hadn't answered Sam. "Virginia," he said. "Back home."

"Virginia!" Sam Raintree shook his head. "With all them Yankee carpetbaggers? What kind of gamblin' can you do in Virginia, pard? Ain't no profit there."

Ivy smiled. He touched the marshal's badge lightly. "What kind of gambling you think you can do here, Marshal?"

"I ain't gotta gamble no more. Got me a quarter interest in the Miner's, and I'm thinkin' 'bout taking over the late Judd Howard's properties come next spring. Be a man of property. That'll help my income as town lawdog, too. Now, answer my question."

"I don't think I'll gamble anymore either, Sam."

The Texan shook his head. "Frank Ivy, carpenter?"

"Most likely. You get rich and decide to retire, Sam, come on to the Massanutton Mountains, and I'll build you a house."

They fell silent, neither one wanting to say goodbye. After a while, Sam pointed to the sign above the door, the one that now read:

Elizabethtown Courthouse and Jail
Established 1869
In Memory of Ian, James and William McKown
Town Marshal: Samuel Raintree

"You reckon the old man would be proud?" he asked.

"Mighty proud," Frank said, holding out his hand.

They shook. Ivy walked down the steps and climbed into the buckboard, his palomino mare hitched to the back with a lead rope. Alice McKown lifted her right hand in parting, and Sam Raintree waved back. Frank urged the team of mules into a trot, Alice leaned on his shoulder and they disappeared down the Cimarron Toll Road.

Marshal Sam Raintree sighed. Not only that, he caught himself sniffing. Well, he was too old, tough and mule-headed to start crying now, so he turned around and put his good hand on the doorknob. Once more, he looked up at the sign.

"Mighty proud," he said, smiling, and went inside.

11/0/